LAUREL

BY
ISABEL
MILLER

THE NAIAD PRESS, INC.
1996

Printed in the United States of America on acid-free paper
First Edition

The quote on page 2, "Everything we vowed we'd never do, we do" is from "Three Views of Eden," by Edward Field. Used by permission.
"O brave new world that has such people in it" on page 6 is from *The Tempest,* by William Shakespeare.
"Has any other watchman stiller stayed to the smiting of this gong?" on page 80 is from May Swenson. Used by permission.

Editor: Christine Cassidy
Cover designer: Bonnie Liss (Phoenix Graphics)
Typesetter: Sandi Stancil

Library of Congress Cataloging-in-Publication Data

Miller, Isabel, 1924 – 1996.
Laurel / by Isabel Miller.
p. cm.
ISBN 1-56280-146-5
1. Lesbians—Fiction. I. Title.
PS3563.I39L3 1996
813′.54—dc20

96-26685
CIP

"No, I loved Manhattan. I always said I'd never leave it except feet first. But as the poet said, 'Everything we vowed we'd never do, we do.' You have to be young and strong to live there. Everything is hard there. Getting food. Getting clean clothes. Going to the doctor. The dentist. In the country everything is easy."

Laurel says, "And you can leave your doors open."

I say, "Do you remember when you and Miles climbed my fire escape and stepped through the big window, very offhand and everyday, but stately? You didn't even giggle. You really carried it off."

Laurel is blushing. That fine light skin shows everything. "I was such a brat," she mumbles. I take her to mean let's drop it.

I guess we both feel we just lately got over being idiots and fear the past.

About the Author

This is Isabel Miller's last book. She died at her home in upstate New York, surrounded by loving friends and family on October 3, 1996, a few days before *Laurel* went to press.

Books by Isabel Miller

NOVELS

Patience and Sarah

*The Love of Good Women**

*Side by Side**

*Laurel**

STORIES AND OTHER SHORT PIECES

*A Dooryard Full of Flowers**

*published by Naiad Press

FOREWORD: NOW

I'm awake all night before Laurel's visit, remembering my follies with her, embarrassed, especially since I was still drinking then and don't even know *all* my follies. But she wants to see me. Does that suggest I wasn't entirely awful? I'll cling to that.

And here she is on my front porch, embracing me and saying, "Dear Lucille, you look the same," which I don't, of course, but she does. She has matured without aging, become solid without thickening. She is a pure and perfect, amazing lovely woman, the same as before, and apparently always will be. She's forty-three now, the same as I was then. I felt so old. Now I see maybe I wasn't.

"Are you okay?" I ask. "Your letter sounded a little strained."

"I'm fine. I was just being shy," Laurel says.

"Shy? With me?"

"Oh, you know—what if you still wanted to be distant?"

"I couldn't possibly hold to that," I say.

She praises my house. "It's a Lucille house," she says. "Everything's different but still the same. Here's the blue rack full of rain hats. What's this big show-offy mahogany desk? I preferred the dinky brown one."

"Beck's got that one."

"Beck! How is she?"

"As fine as most people. Considering that life is almost always sad and difficult. She's made me a grandmother. She sends you her love."

"She was always so beautiful. She looked like you."

"Aw."

"I remember this table. Does one leg still wobble?"

"No. I gave it a new bolt."

"Here's the crock with the blue dragonfly, only now it's full of fresh sunflowers instead of dried teasel. You were a country person in the city. You needed sunflowers and zinnias and lilac bushes and all the stuff you've got now."

"No, I loved Manhattan. I always said I'd never leave it except feet first. But as the poet said, 'Everything we vowed we'd never do, we do.' You have to be young and strong to live there. Everything is hard there. Getting food. Getting clean clothes. Going to the doctor. The dentist. In the country everything is easy."

Laurel says, "And you can leave your doors open."

I say, "Do you remember when you and Miles climbed my fire escape and stepped through the big window, very offhand and everyday, but stately? You didn't even giggle. You really carried it off."

Laurel is blushing. That fine light skin shows everything. "I was such a brat," she mumbles. I take her to mean let's drop it.

I guess we both feel we just lately got over being idiots and fear the past.

CHAPTER ONE: THEN

Miles was my proofreading partner at *Archive* magazine. We sat in a tiny airless office reading aloud to each other. Actually it was the supply closet. He got the job while looking shabby-respectable — the tall, slouchy, young Greek-teacher type. Safely hired, he immediately threw off his disguise. He was in fact the barefoot Philosopher King, come to guide us. No, I was not "losing" Vera; I never "had" her. Nobody *had* anybody. It didn't matter when people used up "my" instant coffee; nobody owned anything. He typed out pages and pages of Bob Dylan lyrics to prove to me they were great poetry. I was touched that he considered me educable. I was a lot over thirty and untrustworthy. I believed in monogamy and baths, but Miles upbraided me like an equal.

Millicent, our boss, called him to her office. He came back saying, “Let the word go forth: shoes will be worn.” I believed in shoes, too. He obeyed in disgusting sneakers that had never known a sock.

In the restroom I saw Laurel, tall but light-boned, with short, straight, dark glossy hair. She was trying to unionize the typists. Such a gentle, soft-spoken firebrand. What a lovely lesbian she’ll be someday, I thought. I considered presenting myself for unionization, even though I already belonged to the Newspaper Guild, but I wasn’t feeling very attractive.

Miles always felt attractive. Through him I could get to know her. I told him there was a revolutionary kid on our floor. Check her out. He wooed her with his all-purpose, never-fail poem. “Stand, Laurel, and be loved,” it ended. He only had to change the name. She started coming around to say she was going out. Did we want anything? She brought me orange juice.

She and Miles came to my apartment unannounced. They climbed my fire escape and stepped through my window shoulder to shoulder as through a triumphal arch.

Vera, thank God, was out.

With Miles listening undismayed, Laurel told me that in a dream she played with my hard nipples, and woke to find they were only the little fluffy knobs on her bedspread. "I was so disappointed," she said.

Nobody in my generation ever said anything like that. We were closed and careful, real turtles. Nobody mentioned nipples. There weren't any.

O brave new world, that has such people in it!

To Vera and most of our friends, the Baby Boomers were ungrateful brats, oversexed and underwashed, having a massive nationwide temper tantrum. To me they were divine and heroic, struggling for an openness and integrity that we couldn't imagine, that had never existed before. I loved their longing to be undefended. Yes, they were arrogant, but gently. Yes, this was the first time in world history that a young man could find a well-brought-up young woman of good family to stick his cock into the moment he could get it up, but they destroyed the market value of the maidenhead. Yes, they did dope, but they came back having seen a world of peace and love. Yes, they were throwing away centuries of Western culture, but maybe a few of them would learn to do electricity and plumbing, and probably they wouldn't forget the wheel.

They were the only force in America standing against Lyndon Johnson and his bombs and then Richard Nixon and his bombs. Congress didn't. The press didn't. Middle America didn't. The Boomers did. For that I would always love them.

Vera told me, "If you could learn to get along with people your own age, you could bridge the generation gap."

She meant I couldn't get along with her anymore. We came together when she decided to and we were ending because she decided to. Our friends felt betrayed. To them we were symbolic.

"Whatever happened to forever?" they said.

"Forever? What's that?" Vera said.

Our life raft had split, she said, and now we needed only to be sure both halves were seaworthy before they drifted so far apart we could no longer help each other.

We had something else to do, she said. She had found at last her real guru, a genuine avatar. He had a halo. He insisted on polarities, opposites. Two women together were like two airplane engines roaring away on the ground with no fuselage. Powerful, maybe, but pointless. I mocked and denounced and cursed him. She commanded me not to speak of him.

I wept. "After all, nothing has happened. Shall we stay the course? Shall we do it all?" I said, forgetting I had cursed her guru. So I should not have said nothing had happened.

I felt like a bug on a pin, spraying tears under her detached spiritual gaze, aloof as a star. All the sweat of human life seemed mysterious to her. Had she spoiled me? One of her bad habits was making herself indispensable. Had she taken a marginally competent housewife and infantilized her? Oh, there was karma there, she feared. Would I ever recover the power to feed and clothe myself? Did I know where the shops were? Did I know my bra size? Could I meet the rent alone on a proofreader's pay, even under rent control? She guessed she should stay, but only as a friend.

"I made a trillion-dollar deal this morning," she used to say. Then, kindly, taking an interest, "And how was *your* day?" But that was before things went bad.

We turned my darkroom into a bedroom for Vera. I wasn't using it anyway. She bought it a hard narrow monk's bed, red curtains, a reading lamp, and a chair. Evenings she went there with her cat, which disliked me, her meditation bench, her rolled-up prayer rug, her book.

"Do as you please in the rest of the place," she said. "Have orgies."

What pleased me was drinking. I was always a drunk. While we were good together I held it down. I thought I was controlling it. Of course she was the one who controlled it, and without her control I just drank.

She still cooked, lots of lentils and green onions for us both. We still had dinner together. One night she said, "I never see you without a glass in your hand."

I said, "Jesus said it does no harm."

"He did not!"

"He did, though."

I found the passage, Matthew 16:11, and read it to her: " 'Not that which goeth into the mouth defileth a man; but that which cometh out of the mouth, this defileth a man . . . Whatsoever entereth in at the mouth goeth into the belly, and is cast out in the draught. But those things which proceed out of the mouth come forth from the heart; and they defile a man.' "

Vera said, "I promise you, what goes into *your* mouth defiles you."

It was only one more harpoon in Moby Dick, one more invasion of Russia, hardly noticeable, but it felt like the last of many last straws.

I said, wearily, "If I can have this place, thank you. If I can't, I'll find another. I want to be by myself."

"I'll start looking," she said, cold as a star.

Maybe Vera had something else to do, create her diamond body or see God or be God — I was never exactly clear — but I didn't, not really. Just humdrum stuff, like take care of myself, live on my pay, until Laurel and Miles stepped through my window like angels alighting and Laurel said, "I dreamed the tufts on my bedspread were your nipples."

Laurel and Miles didn't stay long. They were taking an urban walk.

"I just wanted to tell you my dream," Laurel said, stepping back over the sill to the fire escape.

The capsule of thick gray plastic I'd been in for two years, my full-body armor complete with visor, split like a chrysalis and out I stepped all pink and soft and pretty with something to do: love and be loved. It was not too late.

I would love Laurel. I would love the big square fragrant woman on the subway who carried a box with *lane bryant lane bryant lane bryant* all over it. I would love my haughty aristocratic unfeminist old boss Millicent. Women in their millions I would love, and they would love me back as best they could.

What a treat it was to look into the mirror and see no gray plastic, to see instead a ranch named Bar-None.

At dinner, out of ancient habit, I told Vera. For the first time in two years I amused her, but she went too far. She laughed until she choked and had to go to the bathroom and cough and she came back and laughed again and set aside her plate and laid her head on the table laughing because I was femme and couldn't do any of that. I was timid. My instincts were all hopelessly domestic and monogamous. I was totally incapable of promiscuity, she said, making my jaw sort of drop because she'd never trusted me.

"I want to be there," she said, choking and gasping, "when — you — come — on — to — Millicent!"

Of course I didn't mean, literally, Millicent. I meant I was going to be open, except with Vera. I resolved to keep secrets from Vera and lie to her, as a spiritual exercise. I would stop being a machine for telling the truth and have options.

Laurel and Miles hitchhiked away. She held up her thumb and whenever a car stopped, Miles ran out from behind a bush and climbed in too. They got all the way to California that way and liked it and stayed.

I missed them, even the rich cheesy stench of those sneakers. I was lonely. In a society of couples, a single person, especially a ranch named Bar-None, had no place.

I went to A.P.F.U., A Place for Us, Ap-Fu. I'd always wanted to, but Vera despised it. "Meat wrappers and beauticians and motorcycle riders," she said. "They have fist fights. Not our sort."

Not Vera's sort, maybe, but mine. They did not have fist fights. The rest was true. Dear brave, sturdy, stubborn women holding to what they knew. No guru could have bamboozled *them.*

Of course they had their illusions. One was that someday a rich lesbian would come by and give Ap-Fu a lot of money. Was it me? They knew at a glance it was not.

They lacked the skills of the herd — how to mingle, how to talk small, how to welcome. I kept going back. I needed to sit among their solid bodies. They were the Holy Church of Body Heat. A couple of them liked me. When they kissed me, my mouth was smooth and soft and alive again all the next day.

Laurel phoned from California. She had to come to New York. Could she stay with me a couple of days? Vera still hadn't moved out, but I didn't even ask her. I said yes.

Vera said, "She'll have to sleep with you. Can you behave yourself?"

"No she won't. She'll sleep on the couch."

"I can't do my morning meditation with someone in the living room."

"Do it in your own room."

"No, I'll do it in the living room, as I always do."

The phone rang all day, asking had Laurel come

yet. I began to see that the whole city was in love with her. In the evening the phone rang again. Laurel at the airport about to get on the bus.

"Uh, listen, Laurel, uh," I said, and told her about sleeping with me. "If you'd rather not, uh, I have a long list here of people who want to see you."

Laurel laughed.

"See you pretty soon," she said.

I said, "I will initiate nothing and rebuff nothing."

She said, full of laughter, "Put that in writing."

Her hair was longer. The butchy look I liked so much was gone. We talked most of the night, like a slumber party. I'm guessing. I never went to a slumber party. Snug in the dark under many quilts, with the window open a crack letting in cold spring air, we talked. I was amazed. How could we be so much the same across such differences?

Laurel said, "I always wanted to be best and got real upset if I didn't get all A's. My teachers kept calling my mother to tell her not to push me so hard. They never believed she didn't push me. I'd get back a bunch of papers and search through them till I found something marked wrong and I'd gaze at that and cry."

I said, "Me too, until fifth grade. Then I noticed nobody but the teachers liked me, so I got naughty. I'm not sure it helped."

She said, "The kids *had* to like me. I had two F's."

I said, "I've been considering a really ridiculous step. And probably impossible, too."

"Whatever it is, do it," Laurel said.

"I'd like to try again on adolescence," I said.

Laurel did not laugh, at least not to my face. If she did later behind my back, that was okay.

"Do it," she said.

Laurel said, "I always felt I was so sick and my husband was so well."

"Miles? He's not well!"

"*No!* My *husband*. My ex-husband. He was so perfect, and people wondered why he put up with me, and I agreed."

"Yeah, I've been there," I said.

"But, listen!" she said. "I met somebody the other day who knows him and doesn't like him!"

"Wow!"

"It was so great! It can happen. It can happen to *you*."

"I doubt it. I'm afraid it's not my fate."

Laurel said, "I used to have sexual play with my girl cousins, but when my brother did I tattled on him. I felt it was wrong for him to, but right for me. I always knew, first time I saw you, you were a lesbian. And I wanted so much to tell you I knew and that it was okay. I wanted to tell you I loved you. I kept trying to get Miles to tell me you were, but he was very protective of you and wouldn't tell me. Then he finally said you lived with a woman, and I was so proud of my intuition. I think there should be no partitions in women's restrooms, so lesbians could pick each other up, the way men do."

I said, "I picked you up in the restroom at *Archive* magazine. I mean, I first saw you there and used Miles to get to know you."

"*I* used Miles to get to know *you*. I really liked him. I wasn't insincere with him. But I was always very aware of you at the next desk. Could you tell?"

"No."

"One time when I was fed up with men, I asked my gay friend Seth to take me to a gay bar. It was mixed men and women. I just stood there at the end of the bar and nobody spoke to me until finally an older woman asked me to dance. I got turned on dancing with her, but I got scared because she was so soft. I felt I could be lost in her. She had huge breasts. She was an administrative assistant at Columbia University. Later she called me and I went to her place. We started to make love but I got nervous and she saw I was nervous and stopped and put me into a taxi. She said to feel free to call her."

"Did you?"

"No, but I still might."

"She sounds like a good person."

"Yes. And there's a woman in California. We were falling toward each other. It was going to happen pretty soon. And then I dreamed her house caught fire and her little girl was killed in it and I woke up so scared. I had to call her in the middle of the night to make sure everything was okay. And ever since then, I feel she's a witch trying to steal my soul."

I said, "You were afraid your passion — your fire — would harm her home and family so you retreated. She was passionately approaching passion, and when you stopped, her love turned to bitterness and anger and pain and that's what you feel coming from her now. She's not trying to steal your soul. She's trying to give you hers."

Laurel said, "Men are so much easier. They don't know you have a soul. They just want your body. So they can't really touch you."

"It's your virginity you're keeping," I said.

I said, "In kindergarten I painted a picture of a Dutch windmill and the teacher kept it to send to the fair. So when I told my mother, she said she'd sure like to see that windmill. And I painted another windmill and told her that was it, and then I was guilty for years because I'd lied to my mother."

Laurel said, "Yeah, sure, and I'd have been worried she'd go the fair and see that other windmill."

I said, "I used to think the big gas tank in town would catch fire, and the fire would go through the pipes and into our stove and the whole town's stoves."

"My God, could it?"

"No. It wouldn't have oxygen enough. But I didn't ask anybody. I didn't want my mother to think about it and worry too. She always looked so worried. I realize now that she wasn't. I thought she was worried about our debts, because I was. But she was really very blithe and free. She bought everything on credit, a dollar down and a year to pay — even lamps. Now I won't go in debt for anything — anything."

"Yeah, me neither. My folks put everything on credit cards and paid the minimum every month. I was so scared."

Laurel said, "My mother told me I couldn't go to school if I didn't eat my egg. So every morning I'd sit there in front of that cold egg —"

"Cold? No wonder!"

"Well, it *got* cold. It wasn't at first. And I couldn't eat it. I just couldn't. And every day I believed she wouldn't let me go to school, even though she always did at the last minute."

"Beck wouldn't eat hers, either. So I stopped giving it to her."

"Lucky Beck!"

"Well, people were very shocked. You have to be a proletarian hero to stand against that disapproval. Nobody's persuaded when you say, 'How does it nourish Beck to throw away an egg every day?' Your mother probably thought you would instantly die without that egg and green and yellow vegetables."

"That's exactly what she thought."

"She thought that because she was taught it."

"Well, she could *see* I didn't die."

"It was harder then for women to trust their own eyes."

"It's still hard," Laurel said.

Laurel said, "I was a sexually abused child. They say almost every girl is. Were you?"

"No. One night when I was five or so I slept with my dad, I can't remember why. And my hand fell naturally to my cunt, the way it always did, and he reached over and moved my hand. He not only didn't abuse me, he wouldn't let me abuse myself. That's what they used to call it, self-abuse. I couldn't figure out how he knew. I was quite impressed. I hope I'm not sounding better-fathered-than-thou."

"Oh, it wasn't my father! He wouldn't do that. It was my grandfather. He wanted me to hold his penis. He said he wouldn't love me anymore if I didn't. And I was so afraid he wouldn't love me and would prefer my cousin that I did it. I loved him then, but later I hated him, and when he died I refused to go to his funeral."

When Laurel was little, I thought, her grandfather was probably only about fifty—just a little older than me. I resolved to be the grandfather who could love her whether she touched me or not.

Laurel said, "Did I tell you why I'm in New York?"

"No."

"I have to testify. I was raped. Two years ago."

"Oh!"

"I sort of expected you to say you'd been, too. It's beginning to seem like almost everybody."

"No. I've been spared that. But Beck was."

"Someday when I can stand to, I'll tell you about it."

"No hurry. I'm no more ready to hear it than you are to tell it."

"The district attorney says my sex life weakens his case. I say it should help. It shows I'm not distraught over sex. I'm just distraught over rape. He says the jury won't see it that way. The rapist's been in jail two years waiting for this trial."

"That's unconstitutional!"

"His lawyer won't help him. Hates him."

"I hate him too, but it's unconstitutional."

"I'd drop the charges, but he'd just rape again. He has a history. But the other women won't press charges. I feel I have to do this, for women's sake, because I'm the one who can stand to."

"Yes, you have to."

"I've never had VD, even from the rape," Laurel said. "Have you?"

"No," I said.

"I just wanted to tell you. The DA thought about calling you as a character witness. Then he decided not to. I told him you're large, respectable-looking, a mother."

"Did you tell him I'm queer?"

"No, I left that out."

* * * * *

She fell asleep. Wanting to touch her kept me awake. She half-woke once to say, "I had a thought. Country people are interested in the same things as city people."

"That's a good thought," I said, but I doubt she heard me.

At five of seven, I said, "We can sleep five more minutes," and I found myself able to stroke her hair and shoulders lightly with my fingertips while she told me her dream.

She dreamed she was in her house in California and I was there and her dog was there. She dreamed it two times exactly the same, and it was really nice.

Ah, I thought — her animal is on my side.

At breakfast, Vera said, "I trust you behaved yourself last night, Lucille."

"Yes," I said. "And so did Laurel, but her temptation was not as great so she doesn't deserve as much credit."

Laurel just looked sweet and sleepy.

She came into the bedroom while I was naked, fastening my bra, and watched me dress. I prevented myself from hiding, but feared that the sight of my poor baggy old body with all its scars and stretch marks would be the end of everything.

She said, "Will you let me draw you sometime? You're even more beautiful without your clothes. Nice masses. You have huge breasts."

Not sleepy, not tired, I spent the day catching my

betters in mistakes. I took an unnatural pleasure in their dangling participles, noun-verb disagreements, wrong antecedents. The writers got money, I got conceit. Though lowest of the low, I was smartest.

Laurel met me at the subway. I saw with a *klunk* that she had retreated. Still sweet and friendly, but no longer falling toward me. So I took a tuck in my soul. Exuded some gray plastic. We rode downtown together.

Vera went to her guru. I wrote letters, thinking about alcohol but not quite ready to go buy some. Laurel read. We talked when we thought of something.

She told me the trial was postponed for three months. She'd have to go home and come back again, but what a relief anyway, and what a nice day she had seeing friends, having a sauna at Seth's and a session with Dr. Dane, her old shrink.

Fucking Dane, I thought. Vera had taught me to use obscenity instead of blasphemy to curse with. Miserable, deplorable Dane. He told her I am not a good idea.

Laurel said, "Someday when he's old and needs the money more and I don't need it as much, I'll pay him. He had to ask who you are. You're the only unfamiliar name in my life."

"Who am I?"

"It was all good, what I told him. I said you're someone who'd like me to become a lesbian, but I don't think I will just yet. He told me his wife is unaffectionate and he thinks he married her because his mother was also unaffectionate."

I said, "Do they really pull that shit on *themselves*

too, not just their patients? Are they really willing to bound their souls in that nutshell?"

"I told him you're starting over. He's forty-three, too. Magic age! He thinks his emotional life is over. He wants to learn to be open and affectionate. He's beginning to see that's the way to go."

I said, "I'm beginning to see why people *aren't* affectionate. Because where there's affection, the rest will come too and sometimes it's just not appropriate. Just a bad scene. Like your grandfather."

What was I saying? Was I *threatening* Laurel!

I prayed my tongue might wither rather than threaten Laurel, but it said, "Maybe what your grandfather meant to say was that if he choked his body back, some of his affection would be choked back too."

I was so ashamed of myself.

"Maybe," Laurel said, with a very adult flatness I didn't know her voice could have. It meant *like hell!* "Maybe, but he tried the same thing with a neighbor girl, without affection."

"It was just a thought."

"The women of the family found out about him then, but never told the men."

Ah, she was going on, letting my threat get lost.

She said, "Men seem to need to be unrealistic about their fathers."

"Yes," I said. "My brother thinks our dad was a great man, and I don't point out that he had no great gifts of intellect or spirit. He was a very ordinary ape-man, like everybody else. My brother needs the illusion.

I typed. Laurel read. She was reading John

Humphrey Noyes, the founder of the Oneida Community, on nineteenth-century utopian communities. She and Miles were thinking of starting a commune.

She said, "I hope you were okay last night. I wore a nightgown to make it easier for you. I didn't know if I was going to leap on you or not. Just didn't, as it happened. I hope that was okay."

"Of course. The night made me happy just as it was. I thought you saw that."

"Well, I thought so. But then you talked about my grandfather and I wasn't sure. I told Dr. Dane you're making a whole new loving life and he can too, at forty-three or fifty-three or sixty-three or seventy-three —"

"Maybe not seventy-three."

"— and then he got up and left."

God help me, I thought, now I'm Laurel's shrink as well as her grandfather and the nice administrative assistant with huge breasts.

I said, "Poor Laurel, you turn people on too much."

"Oh, you're so prejudiced against him!"

"Not at all. I identify with him completely. How did it make you feel to have your doctor running in the hall in his surgical gown crying, 'What to do? What to do?' "

"It was okay. He just needed to know I love him, and I do. It makes me sad there's nothing I can do for him, when he's the one who helped me be a real person."

I said, "I just now see the solution to your life problem, which is the fear that people won't love you if you don't put out. Become a shrink, and all your patients will love you but they'll understand that you're bound by law and an oath not to touch them."

"That really makes me mad," Laurel said.

"Sorry."

"I'm so angry. I'm going to Seth's. Okay?"

Clackety-clack. Laurel didn't have to know I was typing nonsense syllables.

She came out of the bedroom with her backpack.

I said, "I'll walk you to the subway. There's some shopping I want to do anyway."

"Is it okay?"

"Stop asking if it's okay. What difference does it make if it's okay or not?"

"You remember Seth's gay. Nothing will happen."

"Let's go."

"His phone's been busy. I have to try again."

I returned Laurel's backpack to my closet. I went back to my desk. She sat down and read. All silently.

At last she said, "You shouldn't have said I'm afraid people won't love me if I don't fuck them."

"I know. I'm sorry. It was stupid and uncalled-for and pompous and know-it-all and not true."

"If it were true, Dr. Dane would have accused me of it. I always expect to be loved. I always feel lovable."

"You are," I said, suffering my own equal and opposite fear, that people would love me and praise me and admire me and be nice to me only if I did not touch them.

Laurel said, "Actually, I think I'd like to be a shrink. You're a good guidance counselor. I think I'll do that."

* * * * *

In bed, Laurel said, "In my dreams, sometimes, I fly."

"Me too."

"I don't flap or anything. I just push down with my right foot and go up. I don't usually go very high."

"Yeah," I said. "One time I dreamed I was in a basement looking into the furnace room. Fire glowing away in there. And three enormous bugs, as big as dogs, came at me. I ran but couldn't run and they were gaining on me and I remembered, hey, I can *fly*. So I flew, just a little. The ceiling was low. But it was enough. The bugs ran under me and away."

Laurel said, "I never remember to use flying to get out of a bad situation. But I can rewind my dreams and make them go right. One time I dreamed my car went over a cliff and I rewound the film and created a bridge and drove across it."

I said, "When I was thinking about leaving Fred and the kids and going away with Vera, I felt so guilty. So unsure I could do it. So grieved. Then I dreamed I was driving on a huge sixteen-lane highway and there was a sign, Toll Bridge Ahead. I had no money, but I couldn't just leave the highway because I was on an inside lane with cars thick all around me. I thought, well, I'll write a check. But I didn't know how much the toll was. I held the checkbook on the steering wheel and guessed the amount and wrote the check. I got up to the toll gate and handed the woman my check. I said, 'I suppose you don't take checks.' She said, 'Sure we do.' I said, 'I suppose it's the wrong amount.' She said, *'It's okay. It's okay. Go ahead!'* and I drove across the bridge. I woke up knowing it was okay to go with Vera. I had paid the price. Even though there'd be grief and pain on all sides, my unconscious would back me up."

Laurel said, "Poor children! I don't want to make you feel bad, but I do feel sorry for them. If you were an ordinary ape-woman, it wouldn't be so bad."

I said, "I thought they were getting a wonderful new mother, warm lovely woman who wasn't a lesbian and wasn't an alcoholic, but she chickened out, even though Fred was the love of her life. She was scared people would say she broke up the marriage. Fred waited a year for her and then married someone else. He had women jumping out of corners at him, lots of choices. He chose a pretty good one. Good for little kids. Not so good for adults. I think nobody's good for both."

"Some aren't good for either," Laurel said.

I said, "One night, when I'd been away about two weeks, I felt such overwhelming grief. I didn't know what to do with it. It was choking me. Then I remembered something Carl Jung said. Telephone your gut, he said. Call it up and ask it, 'Who are you? What do you want? Why are you hurting me?' Then wait for it to answer. Give it a space. It said, 'I am your maternal instinct. You have sinned against the passion that is in all animals to take care of their young,' and I felt lower than a cockroach. I wept. I said, 'But I'm a lesbian. Why does a lesbian have to have maternal instinct?" Then I waited for the answer, but it didn't answer, and after a while it sent up a picture of a pirate flag, black with a white skull. I thought, it's *death!* Is it my death? Is it the death of maternal instinct in me? Or is it calling me a pirate, taking what isn't mine?"

"Did it ever tell you which?"

"No. I watched the flag a long time, and when it faded my grief went away too. It's never been that bad again."

Laurel's breathing got slower and deeper, without the slightest snore, so I phoned my gut. It remarked that I too was quite comfortable, no more lustful, on close examination, than Laurel. "I'm hanging up now. Go to sleep," it said, and I did.

In the middle of the night, I woke from some freeing dream I couldn't remember even then, knowing Laurel wanted me. Knowing.

To see the clock, I reached to the windowsill for the flashlight, and in its sideglow saw also Laurel's eyes, open, bright, calm, sure, looking at me. I put the flashlight back. I slid the window down. I turned the lamp on. Through all that, her gaze held. That lovely tender womanly gaze.

"It's three o'clock," I whispered.

"What's that got to do with anything?"

"I wanted to know, so I thought maybe you did too."

When I stroked her hair and cheek, she suddenly sighed and rolled her head and I was filled with such love that I had to wait and sigh too before I could put my hand under her shoulder and tilt her toward me. We held each other, not even kissing. Everything happened by itself, many times, wave after wave, and afterwards when we were soft and smiling she asked, "What are you thinking?"

"I was thinking I'd like to kiss you all over, and wondering if I could do that without making you think you should be excited, or that I wanted you to be excited. Because it wouldn't be about that. It would be just to say you're beautiful and I love you. Advise me."

"Well, when I first wake up I'm sleepy, and how I feel shouldn't be judged by how I act when I'm sleepy."

"Good," I said, pretending I knew what she meant, "I'll be guided by that," and I kissed her body, saying, "Beautiful beautiful dearest beautiful Laurel." I lifted her hips and held her up to my mouth like a cup. Then I let a pillow do that to free my hands to open her.

She began to work, trying to make the other happen again. But that's a gift. Working doesn't bring it. I couldn't bear to see her work.

"Darling, you don't need to now," I said. "There's no hurry. When I said it was three, what I meant was, it wasn't seven. Maybe we'll wake up again. I'm going to go wash the sleep out of my mouth so I can kiss you."

"You don't need to, Lucille," she said. My name rang in me like a song, telling me I was clean and pure, an angel. So we kissed.

I covered Laurel. I opened the window. We slept pressed together, her silky butt in my lap, my breasts against her silky back. It was five o'clock.

After Laurel, for whom could I ever be unworthy or out of the question?

She dreamed she and I were walking on a beach. I said it was good that the tide was low so we could go really far out. A blue crab caught her toe but I made it stop.

I was calm and happy watching her pack to go to Seth's. She had already stayed longer than she first intended. Beck was due for spring break. There wasn't room in the apartment for both of them.

I said, "Beck doesn't have a key. Would you stay long enough to let her in and give her your key?"

"Sure," Laurel said.

Vera said, "I trust last night was the same as before?"

"I'm afraid so," I said, so proud of being able to lie to Vera. "But it's just as well. I have my period."

I felt so languid and peaceful — full of love, not possessive, not wanting to keep Laurel, not needing to repeat anything unless it fell naturally to us again, not needing to seek anything or mourn anything, not wanting to hold her away from other lovers, just happy.

I've written maybe five poems in my life. Here's the one that came that day:

You pause between my hands.
I hold you a little while,
kiss where your dew is deepest,
admire your rainbows,
pour love to guard your many days,
return you to your long fresh world,
thank God for sending you,

and walk on air.

It felt like a leafy-vine bridge across Generation Gap. I wanted Laurel to know that affection, by taking its natural course, had made me happy — but I wouldn't be a pest. So I sent the poem to her in an official-looking, seriously expensive *Archive* magazine envelope, by the hand of the office messenger. Rank has its privileges.

When I got home, no Beck. She was flying standby, unscheduled. Who knew when she'd get in? And apparently no Laurel either, but John Humphrey Noyes was on the table with the expensive *Archive* envelope, its end torn off, marking Laurel's place.

She called from the bathroom, "I'm having a long, long bath. If someone named Dennis comes looking for me, send him in."

"Okay," I said, wondering why, when you're feeling pretty good, the gods pile something on. Do they have to make you admit, every single day, that you're not so very benign and enlightened and unpossessive after all?

No, they got her out of the tub and dressed while there was still no Dennis. She instantly took up her book. We were very shy and awkward. I don't know if she looked at me. I wasn't looking.

I apologized for her all-day wait. She said it was all right. She enjoyed reading Noyes, making notes for her commune, concentrating on utopian sexual arrangements at the Oneida Community and forgetting to notice child-rearing. Could she borrow the book?

"Yes. Keep it. I don't need it. I gave up my dream of a lesbian commune when Noyes said you have to control the sexual function. You can have communal marriage like Oneida, or celibacy like the Shakers, or anything in between, but you have to have *some* system and enforce it. And lesbians would never obey a system. If we were the obeying type, we'd be straight."

We didn't mention my poem, even though it was sticking out of the book in Laurel's very hands, and I thought, oh shit, she read it in such a blur she didn't see what it said. All she knows is that a poem is serious courtship. She didn't see it was a promise not to be a pest. She's sorry we made love.

Dennis arrived, a sturdy, handsome Columbia student, angry because he'd been offered a job he wasn't qualified for by a man who liked his build. We really had to laugh.

I thought they'd leave right away but Laurel wanted to wait a little longer to meet Beck. Vera arrived and began to boil our lentils. Then at last Beck, my dear red-haired, beautiful, long-legged, ungovernable, twenty-two-year-old first-born child Rebecca, rang the bell and while we watched from the top of the stairs came leaping toward us crying, "What a day! Am I glad to be here! Ma, you old honeybunch! Vera, I was afraid you'd be gone! You must be Laurel! I have to pee!"

Laurel said, "What are you going to do all day while Lucille's working?"

"I don't know," Beck said. "Wander around. See stuff. Sit in the middle of Monet's *Waterlilies.* Ride the Staten Island ferry. Get lost."

"May I come too?"

Beck actually was articulate and had a good

vocabulary, but it failed her then. "Sure! Yeah! All *right!* Hey!"

"I'll come by around nine, okay?"

"Sure! Yeah! All *right!* Hey!"

We watched Laurel and Dennis go down the stairs. Partway down, Laurel turned, looked up into my eyes and smiled her fresh young smile. Safe with Dennis, she could do that. Safe with Beck, I could hold the gaze and smile back.

Laurel was not sorry. No harm done. That was all I needed to know. I was happy. Affection took its natural course and made me happy.

CHAPTER TWO: THEN

When your mother's a lesbian, sleeping with her could feel like sleeping with your father, but Beck unhesitatingly cuddled against me. Our incest barrier was perfect, seamless. Being together was just, no complications, nice.

I tried to tell her family history, but she was tired of those stories.

"This is *oral tradition.* Pretend this is a cave," I said, but she would not have it. She wanted to talk about real stuff.

"Wait till you meet Kirk. You'll love him. He got

bored with his classes and dropped out, to have more time with me. He comes over every day —"

At mealtime, I thought.

"— because I'm exciting and school's not."

I saw Kirk, the mute inarticulate young dropout male American, sitting there in his big sneakers mumbling, "School's a drag, everybody but you's a drag."

I said, "He should be exciting right back at you."

"Oh, he is! He is! He's beautiful, like Laurel, but with a penis."

Thanks to Generation Gap, I couldn't imagine Beck's being passionate any more than she could imagine my being. What looked like a miracle of communication was really just impaired imagination. I had to accept Beck's sex life because she accepted mine.

When she was fifteen, she guessed mine and wrote me a long letter, setting the scene and everything: she was on the stairs looking down into the living room and playing with a cobweb on the ceiling. Fred was in his daddy chair reading the paper, smoking his pipe. Beck said, "I only resent two things about my childhood. One is that you lied to me about Grandpa's cancer." Fred said, "We thought it was too horrible for a child to hear." Beck said, "And you lied about why Mother went away." Fred said, "Why do you think she went away?" Beck said, "I think Mother and Vera are lesbians." Puff puff puff went Fred on his pipe. "You are very observant," he said.

It was an intelligently organized letter. All that came first, then the hope that Vera and I were very happy, then the news that Beck had a lover, but don't worry, they were doing coitus interruptus. Beck pretty much had me cornered into tolerance.

Then I got excited, thinking maybe mothers and daughters could really be *people* for each other, really say something besides that their cold is better and when are you going to get out of that dirty criminal city that's burning up every night on television?

"Yes," Vera said, "but remember how this happened. The daughter has to be the one who breaks through. You couldn't have broken through to Beck. She found your secret and accepted it. You have to find your mother's secret and tell her you accept it."

Either I was never able to find my mother's secret or she kept it to the end. I even asked my dead aunt on a Ouija board. She said my mother felt she had killed her second baby, Douglas, by having intercourse while pregnant. That seemed like a pretty good secret, for my mother's generation, but when I wrote her saying, "I've been thinking about Douglas a lot lately, wondering what he would have been like," as a way of getting the subject going, my mother answered, "I *never* think about Douglas. My cold is better."

Beck said, "Kirk's going to Cuba to help Fidel with the sugar harvest. Then he'll probably have to go underground. Ever since the bomb factory blew up, the Feds are really watching."

The bomb factory was a lovely antique Manhattan town house on West Eleventh Street that some young radicals had an accident in. They blew themselves and it to bits.

I was furious at the people, whoever they were, who had the power to influence and lead this wonderful new heroic generation, who actually got listened to, and who led the children to blow themselves up.

I said, "Beck, I beg you, don't make bombs. Be a little boring. That could have been *your* finger the cops sent to Washington for identification."

"Oh, I'm not going to. I don't want to go underground. I want to work in an orphanage and give all the sad little orphans lots of hugs."

I said, squeezing in a little family history, "One day when all you kids were little, watching TV together, you gave out such a heartbroken howl, such a solid massive wall of grief, that I thought The Bomb had come. I rushed in. No Bomb. It was *Heidi*. And I knew a new generation with heart had been born and the world was okay. And here you are, good baby with a heart, wanting to hug orphans."

I did not tell Beck that I once considered myself an unfailing fount of healing love, too, until the sacrificial life of a heterosexual woman blew me to bits and made me see I was really rather cold and selfish. Maybe Beck was different. She worked part time in a nursing home and liked it. Nothing could be more different from me.

She said, "I pretend the old people are Grandma and Grandpa and I'm getting the chance to help them. I'm not too late. I clean their shit off the wheelchairs and bed rails and the toilet seats and the walkers and the floor. Old people are always shitting. And I think, there there, Amelia, there there, Gus, don't be embarrassed, it's me, it's *Rebecca,* I understand. I have to admit, old people turn me on. They get me hot."

Yes, maybe Beck could hug orphans in droves for years. Maybe she could. After all that shit, mere orphans should be a piece of cake.

Beck said, "I saw these two Chinese women on TV that were Barefoot Doctors, or I guess one was a Barefoot Nurse. And they were all bundled up in big thick padded clothes and riding little shaggy horses in a snow storm —"

"Barefoot?" I couldn't help asking.

"Oh, Mother, don't you know anything? It just means not fancy, not super-trained. The Chinese don't have time for that. So here are these great women, in Manchuria or somewhere, in a snow storm, making housecalls to yurts. And I'm sitting there thinking, gee, I want to do that, I want to be there, I want to be like them, riding little shaggy horses with my friend and helping people."

I felt the doctor and the nurse and the little horses keeping one another warm in Manchuria and I said, "Yeah, me too."

Beck said, "What I always liked about you and Daddy was, you were *equal.* It pisses me *so much* to see him scared of Lee Ann. Scared of making her mad."

I was very curious about Fred's marriage, but I'd made myself a promise to be honorable and never ask about it.

Beck said, "I don't have a room there anymore. Twelve rooms and I can't have one! I don't have any *stuff* there. Remember that old oak drop-leaf secretary you and I bought at an auction for fifty cents? As soon as I started college, Lee Ann said I was adult. She said take my stuff to my adult home, and shit, all I had was a rented room. I had to sell the secretary, but hey, I got three hundred bucks for it. And all my little infantile paintings, Mother, can you keep them till I get a home?"

"Sure."

"I brought them."

"You mean 'The Annunciation,' with the angel with bumblebee wings, and her mouth smiling open like she's got some hot gossip she can't hold one more minute, is *here?*"

"It's in my backpack."

"Oh, I gotta see that angel again!"

Beck's paintings were in a fat brown accordion file. There were lots of them. "Dream Ambulance," "Department House," "The Flight into Egypt," on and on. We were up the rest of the night admiring them.

Beck said, "When I feel depressed, and like I'm an awful person whose own family can't stand her, I go through this stuff and laugh and cry and think about what a great kid I was and pretty soon I think I'm still great, probably, and I'm okay. And I know you love me because you saved it all for me."

"Right," I said.

I lived in some dinky rented rooms myself before Beck got a home of her own. I found space for her file in every one.

Beck and Laurel and a young man named Charles came romping in, laughing, glowing, except Charles, who had the fierce unhappy scowling suspicious watchful face of someone in love. I was glad it was not with Beck, though its being with Laurel was hardly better.

Beck and Laurel had been to the Brooklyn Botanical Garden and seen the magnolias in blossom and the grass full of daffodils.

They rode the ferry and looked at the Statue of Liberty, pretending they were immigrants seeing her for the first time, pretending America really was the promised land, everything wide open and fair.

A street-corner flower vendor gave them red roses, free, because they were what roses were for — beautiful girls happy together in springtime.

Laurel had a date with Charles. He was impatient to go, but she lingered. I stood up to say good-bye and thank them for seeing Beck safely home.

"Tomorrow the Cloisters? Columbia University?" Laurel asked.

"Sure! Yeah! All *right!* Hey!" Beck said.

Still Laurel lingered, looking at me, turning her rose in her fingers, and then she pulled off a petal and gave it to me. I ate it. We smiled.

Beck and I took the TV set to the bedroom, as

far as possible from Vera, and turned the sound way down. We lay and watched four black guys sing and dance, enjoyed their dongs flapping inside their white satin pants, laughed, and then Beck suddenly got up and snapped off the set.

She curled against me, saying, "Do you want to hear about the rape?" The dancers had brought it back.

"I don't know," I said. "Do I?"

"You can take it. It's not violent. I got lost in Chicago and this black guy offered to help me. I suspected him, but I thought how it must feel to be black and have everybody just assume you're a rapist and nobody lets you help them. We got on a bus and went miles and miles through horrible neighborhoods. I decided to get off, even if it did hurt his feelings and make me a racist, but the streets looked so bombed-out and desperate that I didn't dare. He said he lived nearby, let's go up for a minute. I said no, I didn't want to, and he said, 'Okay, here's where we part.' So I went in with him, rather than be left alone there, and he did it to me. He did it to me. I said, 'Let me go, let me go!' and he said, 'But where will you go?' He said, 'Go clean up.' He had a horrible little bathroom with a douche bag. I saw he did this all the time. He had a douche bag. I washed and washed the nozzle, with soap, and douched standing up in his bathtub, and I thought, well, it's okay, if I'm pregnant I'll get an abortion and if I have VD I'll get it treated, and the main thing right now is to get out of here alive. I went back and said, 'I really like the way you fuck! I've learned so much about myself today!' And he became a perfect gentleman. He was practically *courtly*. He took me all the way back downtown. It was still daytime. He took me to the very door I was looking for in the first place. I said thank you."

I just hugged Beck. Held her head against my shoulder and petted her hair.

She said, "At first I felt relieved. Then I began to feel guilty. I didn't fight him. Does it even count as rape when you don't fight?"

"Yes."

"I ended up thanking him. That really gets me. I thanked him. I praised him."

"Never mind. You kept your head and got out okay. That's the main thing."

"I'm afraid I encouraged him."

"Never mind."

"I keep thinking, what if he did that to some really innocent kid that couldn't handle it, and ruined her, thinking he was doing her a favor, because I said thank you?"

"Beck, stay with the facts. They're tough enough. Don't make up anything."

"Am I ruined?"

Her burning question, asked unburningly. Asked rather flatly.

"No."

Her father would have found that guy and killed him. Choked him and dismembered him with his bare hands. For ruining Beck.

"No," I said. "You're a soldier of women's liberation, moving in the world, taking your chances, getting smarter. When I started college, when I was seventeen, the first thing the landlady told us was, 'Don't go out alone. There's been a rape.' It goes way back. Goes back centuries. Time to stop. Time to move in the world and take our chances. You were wounded, like a soldier. That's all. I'm not belittling that nasty experience. But nothing on earth can make me believe it was the end of your life."

Beck said, "Laurel had her rapist arrested. She's going to testify against him."

"Yes."

"I can't do that, because I said thank you."

"Laurel's doing it for you."

"I love her for it."

"Me too."

"Is she a lesbian?"

"No."

"So you just slept together like you and me?"

"Mostly."

"Mostly?"

"One night, briefly, there was more."

"Who did it? Who started it?" Beck asked, hiding her indignation, but not very well.

"Call it a common simultaneous impulse," I said.

"You drove her away!"

"I did not drive her away. She left because we needed the space for you."

"She's been awkward with me. Now I know why."

"If that's awkwardness, we don't need grace."

"I'm afraid now *I'll* be awkward with *her.*"

"No you won't. You can talk about it. It's not a secret, except from Vera."

They were not awkward. They never told me what they said.

I got a letter from another daughter, Beck's sister

Emily, who never came to New York to see me. Fred and Lee Ann would never have forgiven her. They would have considered her lost, beyond redemption, like Beck. But we did write, and talk on the phone. I told Emily family history, the cleaner happier parts. She was only twenty.

In her letter, she thanked me for the history. It made Fred more human, she said — less godlike.

"*Godlike!*" I yelled, so loud Beck almost dropped her cup. "Emily thinks Fred's godlike!"

"Sure," Beck said. "I think he's godlike, too."

"What is so fucking godlike about him?" I asked, my voice trembling with jealousy because she never thought that of me, despite a lot more reason to.

"He's — he's —" and she clasped her hands together and gazed upward, "— he's *Daddy!*"

"Well!" I said. "Well! And if you were fortunate enough to have a god living in your very own home, why didn't you ever do what It wanted you to?"

"Daddy never wanted me to do anything — except not have boyfriends."

I thought of all the things Fred wanted her to do — study, get good grades, be nice to Lee Ann, not get arrested at Vietnam peace marches and anti-nuclear marches, stay away from me — but I didn't mention them.

Could it be, I wondered, that heterosexual women, like men, need illusions about their fathers?

It was time for Beck to go back to school.

"I didn't make you a cherry pie or potato salad, but I did give you good people," I said.

"Right," Beck said. "Now see me to the airport."

"Beck! You want me to ride that awful bus for hours through the bowels of Queens, just to wave at your airplane?"

"Yes!"

"But you've always done that alone, after the first time. I've always been proud of you for that."

"Mother, just this one last time. It's childhood's end. It's childhood's end."

So of course I had to. A guilty mother can say no but not stick to it.

When I got back from the airport, Laurel phoned. She was about to leave for California and Miles.

I said, "You have a letter from California."

"Will you open it and read it to me?"

It was a California poppy, a sprig of lupine, and an Indian paintbrush in a folded paper, no words at all.

"Somebody loves you, it can't be doubted," I said, meaning the witch of course.

"Yes, and I want you to know you're loved too, and you're beautiful," she said.

I said, "Thank you, darling," and walked up to Ap-Fu in the rain, whispering all the way, "Thank you, thank you, thank you, thank you."

On Thirty-eighth Street I saw a hansom cab pulled by a brisk happy horse. I cheered. I was bold about cheering and yelling, from going on peace marches and Gay Rights marches now that Vera couldn't stop me. "Good for you!" I yelled, and the driver tipped his tall silk hat. I thought hansom cabs had to stay in Central Park and this one was making its getaway.

One morning the radio said two ships from the

mass of World War Two leftovers mothballed up the Hudson had broken their chains in the night and headed for the Atlantic. I woke up cheering them, too. I love having something escape, even when it can't get far.

CHAPTER THREE: THEN

A nice Ap-Fu woman named Ardith gave me a ride home every week after the meeting and came up. She was the only one not put off by hearing that my ex-lover still lived with me.

"It's okay, really," I'd say, but only Ardith believed me. She met Vera, who saw instantly that nothing sexual was going to happen. I was slower to see that.

Ardith and I would stay up all night drinking and talking. Most times she wouldn't leave till five, but if she'd kiss me goodnight I could stay awake all the next day and work well, clear-headed and refreshed. If she didn't, I'd have to take a vacation day to sleep. I didn't have anything to do on a vacation anyway.

Ardith was thinking me over, in a neat quiet cautious old-dyke orderly way. Her reckless bed-hopping was twenty years past. Forty-five-year-old lesbians are so tired of drunks and getting up in the cold to go home. I answered all her questions, confessed all my crimes and follies, and bragged where possible.

I was not easy to choose. On the one hand, a kind heart, on the other hand, alcohol addiction. On the one hand a tendency to bond, on the other an ambition to bar none. A high IQ but a lousy job. A good vocabulary but a bad figure. A really good photographer, but no sales.

Sometimes Ardith gave a hint about which way she was tending. She said, "You're still too much of a 'we' with Vera."

I learned to leave Vera out of my stories and say, "*I* went to Susan B. Anthony's house in Rochester," and so on. But Ardith knew very well I was still *thinking* "we." How could I not?

She said, "Your life with lots of love but not very much sex is really better than most people's, which is lots of sex but not very much love."

She said, "You seem to admire promiscuity."

"No," I said. "I admire the struggle to be undefended."

She said, "I think you don't know what's out there."

I didn't. I'd been to bed with one man and three

women in my whole life, and one of the women was Laurel. That's how much I knew.

But I was almost willing to go back into monogamy without having made a dent in my ignorance, and I think Ardith was almost ready to take a chance on me. I never found out for sure, because one night while we were talking at 2 a.m., the phone rang.

"Lucille!" it said. "I sent you a message to be up."

"Laurel!" I said.

"Can you talk?"

"Yes!" I said, not caring that Ardith did not budge, stayed right there listening. The phone was in the bedroom but I felt it would be rude to close the door.

Laurel said, "I've been thinking about everything we did."

"Me too. A lot."

"You and I loved each other so much, so fast," Laurel said. "I keep wondering, why was I so *shy* with you? I'm not that way with anybody else."

"We were both shy," I said.

"It was *terrific* with you. It was amazing."

"Yes, it was beautiful."

Laurel said, "The only thing that pissed me was, you did it to me, and I was planning to do it to you. Why couldn't I tell you that? But now I can. I want to talk about it."

"We can do that," I said.

"Lucille, I have to be in New York in three weeks, and I'd like to stay with you again. Is that okay? We can talk about it then."

"Yes, but Vera will still be here. Is that okay?"

"Oh, sure. I like Vera. Even though she does seem to think you're slightly retarded."

"I mean, the same bed shortage."

"I'd want to sleep in our bed anyway. Why is it so hard to say that, when it's you? To other people I can say, 'Want to fuck?' But when it's you and I say, 'Our bed,' I blush."

"We can work up to it. How's your witch?"

"Pretty good. I'm going to give her a kiss on Sunday. And there's someone else who was really depressed about being fat, but now I know, *it doesn't matter.* And I proved to her she's beautiful. I'll tell you all about it in three weeks. The moon and one bright star are rising. I love you."

"I love you too."

When I put the phone down, I jumped up and paced, elated and scared, wondering out loud if I could give this love its exact value, set it neither too high nor too low. And could I lose a couple of pounds in three weeks? And did I dare upgrade our night from sweet and dear, affection taking its natural course, to *terrific, amazing?* Yes! If Laurel said so, I could say so. I had permission.

Ardith, who already knew a moderate sensible version of Laurel, watched me pace, listened to my little ecstatic remarks, and said, "I don't understand you. Are you going to settle down with Laurel now?"

"Oh no. That would be inappropriate. We'll make love while she's here and then she'll go away and I'll just be her good-mama friend for the rest of my life."

"And yet you want to lose weight."

"Laurel is twenty-three, and beautiful beyond belief, beyond reason, and I'm forty-three and not a well-preserved forty-three, and yeah, I'd like to sharpen up a little."

"She'll be sleeping with other people while she's here. With men. And that's all right with you?"

"I'd rather she didn't. But it's none of my business. My business is what happens when we're face to face, and if that's clear and right, then, yeah, what she does elsewhere is all right with me."

"You do mystify me," Ardith said, and left two hours earlier than usual, without a kiss. I think it's safe to say she was only minimally disappointed or hurt, thanks to always keeping her guard up, her careful management. But she was mystified.

And I was scared. How was I going to keep Laurel's embrace from meaning too much? How would I stay calm and busy when she was with someone else, and happy to see her, not reproachful, when she came back? I needed my feeling diluted. I needed the help of a sexy pal.

I called some women who had flirted with me before when Vera wasn't looking, but they were newly in love or in a tight relationship or leaving town or cautious on hearing Vera was still around. And Ardith's decision was made at last: no. Which was all right. She would not have helped. She would have outlawed Laurel entirely.

There was no help. I would have to be, full-force, idiot or angel or old goat or wilting flower without distraction.

Laurel climbed the stairs. I waited at the top. My arms were full of Vera's struggling cat, which always charged the door, so I couldn't hug Laurel hello. But I did glow a welcome at her.

She smiled politely. I saw she had changed her mind.

She was sorry about the phone call. All my dilemmas flew away, and wasn't I better off without them?

Vera put supper on the table. Laurel said, "I can't eat. The trial begins tomorrow. I've been at the district attorney's all day. He seems so unsure. He chose a jury of blue-collar workers, and now he thinks they're worse. Aren't they the ones who think women are asking for rape? He kept wanting to know what I think. I don't want to think. I want *him* to *know*. He kept making me go over and over my testimony until I cried and then he scolded me for crying. Then he thought maybe I *should* cry. Maybe the blue-collar people will be touched. I'm all in a knot. I can't tell you."

Vera studied Laurel as she used to study me, back when she took care of me. She had a gift for seeing what was needed. "You need something orderly and austere, to remind you there's something above and beyond all this," she said, and put some Bach on the record player. We listened.

"That's so nice. Are you going to think I'm an ungrateful brat if I still can't eat?" Laurel said, not noticing that she was popping a tiny bright tomato into her mouth. She laughed and popped another.

But she got a phone call. She came back saying, "I told Charles he could come down for a little while."

I said, "You're tense again already, and he hasn't even glowered at you yet."

"Oh, he's upset. He's got this stomach problem that nobody can diagnose. Another doctor today couldn't. So I had to say okay. But I said *a little while.* He won't stay long."

He must have called from a street phone in the neighborhood, he was there so fast. Vera and I politely left him and Laurel alone in the living room, isolating ourselves from the record player and the TV and books and magazines and desk. We waited on kitchen stools for him to leave. Vera closed her eyes and meditated. I sipped some Scotch. We waited.

Waited and waited on kitchen stools. I began to hate Charles. Toward the rapists I could almost feel a certain tiny socioeconomic forgiveness, but Charles I hated. I hated him in fifteen-minute increments, more each time our clock chimed the quarter hour and the Metropolitan Life clock tower bonged.

Vera said, "He's being very insensitive, making sexual demands on someone who's facing a trial about sex."

I said, "He's getting germs all over her and giving her an undiagnosable stomach disease."

The Met Life clock bonged again and pushed my hatred to a hotter degree, but I just sat there on the kitchen stool. It was Vera who said, "Since Laurel seems unable to send him away, I will."

I could say, well, Vera didn't have to be afraid of looking jealous, and what did she care if Laurel got mad? when the fact is, I was a wimp.

It was many years since Vera was a professor, but she remembered how to daunt young men. Appropriately subdued, Charles stumbled to the door and left. I wish I knew what Vera said to him. I hope she called him a no-good son of a bitch for hassling Laurel on a night like this. (What do we call those people now that we don't want to offend bitches?) She probably just gave him a quelling glare and said, "It's time for you to go."

I had to love Vera then. I had to be proud of the many years she loved me.

Laurel took a long perfumed bath by candlelight. I sat on the toilet lid enjoying the beauty of her dim wet body, as I would have enjoyed a sunset or an apple orchard in bloom, feeling peaceful. Laurel seemed peaceful too, not hiding, not shy.

She said, "Once I got lost in a place I knew every inch of, because there'd been a hurricane. All the landmarks were blown away. Houses. Trees. Everything. And I thought how powerful nature is, and how we don't really need to worry about harming anything as powerful as that. All our little pollution and stuff, that we worry about — whenever we go too far — whenever nature notices us — all she has to do is swing her tail like a huge crocodile and just wipe us out. We'll just be extinct, and serves us right."

If Laurel could let me look at her, and if she would tell me her wonderful original thoughts, that was lovemaking enough. It made me happy.

"Yes, but I don't want you to be extinct," I said.

We went to bed. I wanted nothing but to keep her calm and well-rested for her ordeal. I decided to read the encyclopedia to her until she fell asleep.

"Listen, listen to every word, concentrate," I said. "It will shut off the squirrel cage in your mind."

"All right," Laurel said, unconvinced.

“ ‘Agriculture,’ ” I read. “ ‘The art, science, and industry of managing the growth of plants and animals for human use,’ ” and so on. When I was about eight inches down the page, Laurel rewarded me with a soft buzz. She was asleep.

She woke briefly and said, “I’m dreaming I’m in my house in California. A lot of women are in my house expecting tea. But I didn’t invite them. They won’t go away. They’re nice, but they won’t go away.”

Yes they will, I thought. We’ve already gone.

Next day was trial day, no more postponements. Laurel put on pantyhose and her only dress, which she’d saved in case she had to go to a funeral, knitted nylon navy blue with a white collar. Fortunately, it was not super short. It reached mid-calf. No one could imagine she was asking to be raped.

“Lucille? I need your advice? Do I look more respectable with my hair down like this? Or pulled back — like this?”

“You look virginal with it down. But militantly virginal with it back.”

She clipped it back.

At breakfast she asked, “Does anyone know a good prayer to get me through today?”

“ ‘Nothing inharmonious can enter my experience,’ ” I said, but what did I know about getting the Universe to give me what I wanted? My record was awful.

Vera, whose record was excellent, said, “That’s putting it negatively. It needs to be positive. Like this: ‘Only harmony can enter my experience.’ ”

While I was sitting on my bed pulling on my

pantyhose, Laurel came in and gave me a quick fresh kiss on the lips.

I smiled. "Only harmony can enter your experience," I said.

I want to celebrate a great unsung milestone in women's history, and the great unsung hero of it all, Ingrid Bergman's beautiful daughter Pia Lindstrom. Well, she's sung for beauty and brains, but I sing her for wearing slacks to work at CBS at a time when "creative" men at CBS wore torn jeans and didn't shave, and any woman who showed up in slacks was sent home to put on a skirt. But CBS couldn't send Pia home, not Pia, and she broke the wall for the rest of us.

Even *Archive* magazine, even Millicent, who came to work in a hat and gloves, had to notice. Millicent was stubborn. There was a kid in the art department Millicent sent home every day to put on a skirt.

I said, "She rides her bike to work. A skirt flies up over her head. She gets lewd comments."

"Are you sure she minds?" Millicent asked. She was so tough. I marveled at my earlier plan to embrace her.

I said, "These kids have been in pants since they were born. Pants are just clothes. They're freedom. There's nothing masculine about them. They're just comfortable clothes shaped like a body, as a shoe is shaped like a foot."

Millicent said, "Pantyhose are shaped like a body."

"They generate static electricity. They're expensive. They get runs. Pants last for years."

"Why should any woman want trousers? They chafe me," Millicent said.

There was no budging her. Women in other departments started wearing pants to work, but we could not.

It was on that first day of Laurel's trial that Millicent called a staff meeting. We were mostly middle-aged women. *Archive,* like most other businesses, depended on liberally educated middle-aged divorced women who were too grateful for a job to be any trouble. There we stood all timid and grateful with our dresses plastered to us by static electricity as though soaked with water, and there stood Millicent, former Navy commander, in her dress, proclaiming emancipation.

"Trousers may be worn!" she cried. "And I don't mean this for just the young and shapely. The lid is *off*!"

Later I went to her office and thanked her. "This is the morale equivalent of a twenty-five-dollar raise," I said.

"You wait, you feminists, you wait until men start treating you the way they treat each other. Then you'll see."

I saved one dress and one set of pantyhose in case I had to go to a funeral.

Vera said, "If Laurel's going to stay any length of

time, she'll need to chip in some money. But she's a fine child. I think she'll want to. I ain't supportin' *two* women I don't get no nooky from."

It was a little jab but it touched my bones. "You don't support me! I pay my share!" I said, weeping.

She was sorry. She had tried to make a little joke and miscalculated. It was intended to be shallow and absurd, not mock my fear that I couldn't take care of myself alone. She was sorry. "Forgive blunder?" she asked. I didn't forgive it, but I buried it deep enough to let us resume our smooth surface. Enough to let us live in the same space for another three weeks.

Laurel phoned to say she was having dinner with Charles and might be out late. I was reading in bed when she and Charles came in. They sat on my bed, confident of Mama's welcome, as in the lovely slow Sunday mornings of childhood we've all heard about.

Vera, who was supposed to be asleep, called me to the living room. "They let the cat out," she said.

"I'll scold them."

"And I don't want to find that miserable boy on the couch in the morning."

Vera was so smart. Charles did ask to stay, sure enough. I said, "Sorry," and blamed Vera.

We talked about our demons. They can be recognized by their will, which is not our will.

"I don't have any demons," Laurel said.

I said, "I think maybe you really don't. Your face would show them if you did." Her face showed angels.

Charles said, "I have demons."

"Yes," I said. "I see them in myself, and I see them in you." They had taken over his face entirely.

He had one of those lean, pale, thin-lipped faces

that stay the same from about age fifteen to about sixty. His teeth were so far inside they barely showed when he smiled. He could have been a Grand Inquisitor, a Nazi, a hangman, an assassin, a saint, but he was merely a mathematical genius. Weren't they supposed to be all brain? Why was Charles fiercely, angrily, hugely, sloppily, moochily in love?

Maybe Mathematical Charles wanted to leave, but Demonic Charles did not. He kept leaning toward Laurel and groaning, not leaving even when Laurel yawned and said how tired she was and that she'd see him tomorrow. He could not keep his hands off her, though she leaned away.

Is it testosterone that makes men believe that God's plan is for them to have anything they want?

"Charles," I said. "Charles, it's late."

"It's all right. I quit my job," he said.

"I didn't," I said.

Where was Vera now that we needed her?

I became Imitation Vera, saying, "It is time for you to go," each word separate and distinct, no backtalk possible. "And don't let the cat out."

Charles did go then, slowly, to give me a chance to repent. Laurel went along to hold the cat in. I expected another long delay, but I guess Charles did not dare, right outside Vera's bedroom door, which was open for the convenience of the cat. Laurel was soon back, fresh-washed and naked inside a big T-shirt.

"He's so tiring," she said. "I'm sorry I let him come up. I didn't think he'd stay so long. He came to the trial. I asked him not to. He was there all day. I didn't want anybody I knew there. He thought he was supporting me. Someday I'll tell you about the trial. I really did cry. I didn't have to fake it. I feel I'm on trial and they'll find me guilty. It was stupid to let Charles come up when I'm so close to freaking out. Why are you upset tonight?"

Rather than let her think I was jealous of Charles, I admitted, "Vera and I quarreled."

"I feel Vera likes me," Laurel said, knowing at once we'd quarreled about her, "but I could blow the whole thing with one misstep."

"That's true," I said. "But you have not yet made a misstep."

"I shouldn't have let Charles come up. The door was fantastically loud. I left some household money on the table."

It's really nice to deal with people who get things without having to be hit over the head.

"I'm going to read to you," I said. "'Aerodynamics, the branch of fluid mechanics that deals with the motion of air and other gases,'" and so on. She was soon asleep, and so was I.

Again she kissed my lips goodbye. Again I said, "Only harmony can enter your experience," and smiled.

She came home without Charles, and in time for supper.

Vera went to her meeting. Charles phoned. I wrote letters. I watched television a little. Charles phoned again. I did some hand laundry, and while I was at it I also washed Laurel's virginal blue nylon dress, which she had left beside the bathroom sink for washing. Laurel cleaned up the kitchen. The phone rang.

"It's Charles," Laurel said, "to explain why I should go to bed with him. But I won't." She picked up the phone. "Hello again," she said. "Hello, Charles."

I thought about Charles and how little put off he was by Laurel's anger or boredom or avoidance or embarrassment, how ready he was to whine and cling and importune, how like a spear he set his will on her, and the will of his demons too. Did he not care about Laurel's feelings, or did he not feel them? Or did he feel them and only grow more angry and determined, the fierce mastering male straight out of D.H. Lawrence, who would make her pay for driving him to slimy contemptible devices? And what did he think he'd have in his hands after a reluctance like Laurel's? Or didn't he care, just so he got her? Or was Charles really a nice guy with demon trouble?

Laurel came to wash her dress. When she found it dripping from the shower rod, she said nothing — but I felt her annoyance. I felt she thought me meddlesome, an intruding mother who now expected a reward.

I resolved not to intrude anymore, beginning with not reading to her, not making sure she slept. Looking like hell in court would make the jury feel protective anyway.

We went to bed. She wanted to talk, but not our old anecdotal personal stuff, preposterous exchanges across Generation Gap. To my dismay, she wanted to talk about *me*.

"You don't like yourself, and why don't you?" she

began gently. Everything she said that night was gentle.

"Actually I do like myself," I said.

"I feel you don't. I think you feel incomplete, but why?"

I had no ready answer. "I hope I'm not complete. I hope there's more to me than this," was all I could manage.

"You're unhappy," she said, and I obediently became unhappy, thinking, yeah, it was tough having to give up my idiotic fantasies, yeah, I was disappointed, and I should have the guts to admit it but I am of an older, more cowardly and guarded generation and I won't admit it.

"Do we have to talk about this right now?" I asked.

"Yes! Because I feel I'm what's making you unhappy."

"Well, you're not. I have a complex life with a lot going on, and if I'm unhappy — which I deny — it has nothing to do with you."

She said, "I feel you're expecting something from me that I can't give."

I felt like Humbert Humbert trying to comfort Lolita, and his erection prods her and she cries, "Oh, God, not again!" or like Fred trying to comfort me, but I felt the injustice of being accused of an erection when I did not have one. My desire was dead. I strangled it, I strangled it, couldn't Laurel see?

But I also knew she was upset from the trial and wanted to hurt somebody, and she chose me because I was the one she trusted most.

She said, "I just can't do anything when somebody expects me to."

"Um," I said.

Laurel said, "You feel incomplete and you're trying to use sex to complete yourself, and I don't want to help you complete yourself that way. Say something!"

"Um," I said.

"And you're too nice. There's something almost manipulative in your niceness. You're kind and nice so people will like you. I had a long talk with Vera and she agrees with me. She said she used to be nice so people would like her, but now she's just herself and people like her better."

I said, "It was the opposite for me. Back when I wasn't nice, people didn't like me. Then I became nice and they did."

Laurel said, "Vera loves you. She told me so. But you're kicking her out because it isn't sexual anymore. You are so much loved, and you don't even notice it. You just brush it aside. It's just the atmosphere. You just take it for granted, like the atmosphere. You should let it make you happy instead of wanting sexual things to complete you."

"Do you mean I shouldn't want sexual things, or everybody shouldn't?"

"I think I mean *you* shouldn't."

A huge unexpected tear-bladder began to empty through my eyes, but my voice stayed okay and I hoped Laurel wouldn't notice. I said, "Yes, well, go to sleep. I have to make a phone call."

"Will you wake me when you're through?"

"No."

"Then I won't go to sleep."

I phoned the tangle in my gut, asking, "Who are you? What do you want? Why are you hurting me?

What are your terms?" I lay waiting for an answer for a long time but did not get one.

"Are you through with your call?" Laurel asked.

"I guess so. The operator asked for another dime."

"What did it say?"

"Nothing much. Ashamed of itself, I suppose. I'm going to sleep now."

"I want you to answer me. I want a *conversation.*"

"Not tonight." I couldn't keep the hamminess and tightness out of my voice, but at least I didn't sob.

I was distantly aware that Laurel was weeping too, but I had to concentrate on my own problems. I waited until I hoped she slept and then I got up and anesthetized myself with Scotch, plain pure burny Scotch, which never gave me a hangover. It's when you put a lot of garbage — oranges and cherries — into your scotch that you get a hangover. Correctly numb, I crept back in beside Laurel and fell asleep. No wonder the Greeks made a god of alcohol.

Nevertheless, in the morning I woke up weeping. I put ice on my eyes and made my getaway before Laurel even woke up. To hide my eyes, I wore my reading glasses all day, not just to read. The sweet kid from the art department, who believed I was the cause of her being able to wear pants to ride her bike to work, made me a little cheer-up card. It may have helped some. I taped it to my lamp. Laurel was right — I lived in a sea of love.

I phoned Vera, who was very busy with something major she was not at liberty to reveal. "I want to sleep on the couch tonight," I said. "Would that interfere with your meditation?"

"Not as much as an outsider. But of course it would make a difference. Why do you want it?"

"I just do."

"What happened? Why should I make this—adjustment? I almost said sacrifice."

"Nothing happened. I just want to."

"For how many nights?"

"I don't know."

"Oh, you *are* mysterious! But all right," Vera said.

I don't think I fooled her. She too got things without being hit over the head. Sometimes that's a nuisance.

Vera had to work late. Laurel was lying on the floor, very tired, when I got home. She said the trial was almost over and she had only to be on call now. "Is it all right if I lie here?" she asked.

I laughed, unkindly, and didn't answer. In the course of the day I had achieved anger. Laurel had made my feelings seem absurd, as though Santa Claus or Dwight D. Eisenhower should get the hots. Anger may be negative, but it comes in handy. I said, "I'm going to sleep on the couch tonight."

"Why?"

"Because I don't like your feeling that you're being pressured sexually."

"Couldn't I sleep there?"

"Vera couldn't do her meditation."

"Why can't we sleep in the same bed?"

"That's what we *were* doing and it felt like sexual pressure to you and I don't know any other way to end it."

She stood up and left the room. I heard her dialing the phone and felt great grief. Anger gone, tears back. She hurt you, I thought — be *angry,* you wimp! I went to the bedroom. She was packing.

"Where are you going?" I asked.

"To Seth's."

"I would feel very bad to think I drove you away. Could we talk? Have you told Seth yet?"

"No. He doesn't answer. Maybe I'll try Charles."

"First let's talk."

We sat at the table. She said, "I have to go, to keep from spoiling everything. If I go now, I can come back sometimes. I've made you unhappy."

I said, "I was happy until last night."

"You didn't look it."

"I was, though. I just delight in you, as Vera does in the cat. Ignore these tears. I cry easy."

"I feel I'm disappointing you and making you unhappy, but I can't do things when people expect it. The trial is making me feel that I invited the rape. Maybe I come on sexually with everyone."

I said, "You never came on sexually with me," which was almost true, true enough for this conversation.

"I'd like to think I didn't," she said. "For such a long time I wanted to give you my body" — she used that actual quaint wording — but when the time came I couldn't do it."

"When did you want that?" I asked.

"From a little while after I met you," she said, making my tears stop on the spot. The point was not to be someone who shouldn't want anything like that.

I said, "It never crossed my mind. I thought of you as a child —"

"I'm a grown woman."

"— and it never *would* have crossed my mind if you hadn't unexpectedly turned up in my bed, and then it did cross my mind."

Laurel said, "I have some sexual feeling for everyone I care about."

"I do too, but in my generation we just block that out, and I thought it was so great, the brave new world where you could let your love have some sex in it. Our embrace was an accident — not part of my natural life course — and it was a miracle and very sweet and, to me, *good,* but then next day I saw you were sorry."

"I wasn't sorry," she said, without saying what she was.

I said, "It wasn't passionate or deep, but very sweet."

"I thought you were disappointed because it wasn't passionate."

"I wasn't passionate either. You must have noticed. When you were leaving with Dennis and looked back and smiled at me, I felt that was enough. I saw that you loved me again, and that was the happy ending."

Laurel said, "Yes, I felt that too."

I said, "Then you phoned me at two-thirty one morning and said you *liked* it, and I thought, wow, if you like it I can like it. And then you came back, and I saw at a glance nothing physical would happen, but you let me look at you and told me your thoughts and dreams and that was lovemaking enough. I was happy. And I thought you *knew* that. I thought you could see."

"I was too self-engrossed from the trial. I wasn't looking. Otherwise I would have seen."

I said, "Maybe my refusing to talk in our old way, and just reading you right to sleep felt like sulking and heavy breathing."

She said, "The reading was really nice, but awfully boring. I would rather have talked."

I said, "It really hurt me when you said I — like it was me alone in all the world — I shouldn't hope to be completed by sex."

"Well, you hurt me when you said I'm afraid people won't love me if I don't give them my body. And I'm afraid I do think that. I came to realize. I started noticing."

"People will love you anyway," I said.

"You should definitely expect to be sexually loved," she said, and we laughed. We didn't believe each other, but our feeling was mysteriously sweet again.

Vera came home and burned a rope of Tibetan incense to cleanse the living room. I said, "I can't possibly sleep with that sicky smell."

Laurel smiled. She never did say she'd stay, but she stayed. While she was on the phone with Charles, which was most of the evening, I returned her backpack to the closet. I was getting good at that. We slept together.

* * * * *

The next afternoon Laurel called me at work to say, "The jury found me not guilty."

"Hooray!" I said.

"The rapist is going to prison. He can't lie in wait for me in the dark."

"Thank God."

"So Charles and I are going to celebrate and stuff, and it could get pretty late, so I think I'll just stay at his place."

"Okay," I said, thinking, O thou who canst do nothing somebody expecteth!

She said, "I happened to mention to Charles that I've never seen the Liberty Bell or any of that patriotic stuff, so he's going to take me to Philadelphia."

"Why Charles? Where are all your other friends?" I asked, crossly, knowing where they were. Charles drove them off. To see her they had to see him.

"Well, they've all got jobs. He's the only one with time during the day."

"God, I hate it when these shitty devices work," I said. "He's mewled and puked at you until you consent. Why are you afraid of a nice old lady you love, and not afraid of a demonic young man you hate?"

She answered so softly I had to listen twice to hear: "I'm afraid you want to steal my soul."

At first I thought I wouldn't dream of it, and then I thought, well, maybe in a certain way I do want to. I want her whole insides, her thoughts, everything that makes her Laurel, and maybe that's her soul. And maybe, I thought, she's not wrong about her poor young witch friend in California, either.

Laurel said, "Charles knows people in Philly. So maybe we'll stay a few days."

"Okay," I said.

"So I'll see you next week. I'll let you know. But not for long. I'm really missing Miles."

"Okay. See you," I said, wishing I could be more Miles and less grandfather and shrink and administrative assistant and witch. My problem was personal. Some young hotheads at Ap-Fu kept trying to tell us our problems were political, but I knew mine was personal. I'd simply missed out for this incarnation. I'd wasted my youth and beauty on Fred. The world got brave and new too late for me. I wondered if I could go back through the calendar and snip out the day of my birth. I didn't want to die. I wanted never to have been.

There was a man on the subway announcing that he was "old, crippled, and ready to die — seventy-nine years old." He played, not well, "The Halls of Montezuma" and "Onward, Christian Soldiers" on a harmonica and sang. He was white, clean, not in terribly bad shape if he really was seventy-nine. He made me see there were still lots of things between me and death besides love. There was pride, of which he had freed himself. There was the fear of being a public fool and nuisance. Lots of things. Apparently he was begging. At least some people gave him money. I was really surprised when he took it. I thought he was making some kind of spiritual statement, what an old Eskimo might say before going out to freeze.

* * * * *

In a bar I met someone entirely unsuitable and took her home. We went to bed drunk and woke up thirsty. Vera, meditating in the living room, caught me fetching orange juice and wept because I'd never done that for her. My temporary friend stole away without asking to see me again. I was relieved.

Vera, sobbing, said, "I see now what you'll do for sex. I see now sex is all I ever meant to you, and all the wonderful things were just something to pass the time until sex."

"Oh, cut it out," I said, quite hung over. Her tears never moved me, because they felt like a temper tantrum.

She sobbed, "You have rubbed my nose in your erotic life and I'm jealous."

I thought of all the women who had backed off when they heard my ex-lover was still around, even though I explained that she cared not a whit for me anymore. How did they know Vera, sight unseen, better than I did?

"You thrust your own nose into my erotic life, and please take it out again," I said.

"You don't need to do sordid things," Vera sobbed. "If you need something, you can ask *me.*"

That stopped me. It caused me to produce an amazed sound. I had asked her so many times. No wonder she despised sex if she thought she could get me back with it.

I said, "It wasn't sordid. She was a perfectly nice woman. She took my tears away."

I had a single simple humble focused ambition, to say good-bye to Laurel without tears. And because of that embarrassing night, I succeeded. Thank you, unsuitable woman.

CHAPTER FOUR: THEN

Vera said we would split everything down the middle, including money. I said that wasn't fair to her, because she always earned more than I did. Then she started going to fancy auctions and buying brass objects and gorgeous Asian carpets, and I sort of gulped but kept still, trying to force myself to be fair.

But one evening she asked how much was in my savings account. She was calculating how much each of us would get.

I said, "I thought you'd changed your mind about all that."

"What made you think that?"

"Oh — auctions and stuff."

"What I have spent at auctions is less than the difference between our weekly salaries. As things are now, we should each get about three thousand dollars. I think you'll find you need it while you learn to live without my salary."

It took me years to stop being stingy and scared.

I helped her pack, sneaking in all my least favorite records, such as "Drums of Passion." She gave me almost everything, even stuff she had before we met. She wanted to change her style — sleep on a mat she would roll up every morning, sit on those carpets, eat off a huge round brass tray, wear paper slippers. She wanted no books except her mystic ones. She left me the slides of our life together, even the ones of the cat being cute. She left our love letters in my filing cabinet.

Even so, with what little she did take boxed up beside the door and just one picture down from the wall, the soul went out of the place.

The movers were to come the next day. I was going to an Ap-Fu meeting.

"You're going *out?*" Vera cried.

Fine time to get sentimental, I thought.

I said, "I can't bear to sit here in the ashes of our home."

"I can't bear to sit in the ashes of our home alone, Lucille," she said.

I stayed. We sat together on the couch. I had not looked at her in so long. When I saw more gray in her hair than I remembered, and new little lines around her eyes and how tired she was, I wept a little. I apologized for cursing her guru. She apologized for being tough and hard against my loneliness.

She said, "I want you to know that in the light of what I'm learning now, it was the least unkind of the alternatives available."

I thanked her for being ruthless enough to break me away from Fred. She thanked me for erasing her cruel mother with a new infancy, stories and songs and piggy-on-the-toes and dressing and undressing and baths. I thanked her for the new childhood she'd given me, the little racing cars whizzing around their track, the games of jacks, the Twinkies, the bubble gum, the guessing games, and Doctor and Beauty Parlor and Pull Down the Pants and Whisper in the Ear.

Vera's new place was uptown, near her guru. It had a doorman. I expected to put up her shelves and curtain rods, since like most butches, she was bad with tools, but she said the men from her group would do that. It really gave me a pang to think of her believing in proper gender roles and all that. Men drilled and screwed. Women cooked and sewed.

She came back every few days with a shopping bag from which she extracted four or five of my unfavorite records, until I had them all back, and a length of cloth she was making something large and simple out of, something Asian or Arabic or perhaps a shroud. I didn't ask.

She sat there with her proud butch neck bent at the sewing machine making panic noises and not many stitches. I taught her not to have her foot on the pedal when she threaded the needle, and stayed in the next room. I didn't like to see her neck bent, and I didn't like what was first a suspicion and then a certainty: my Vera, who went crazy with the tickling if her hair reached halfway to her collar, was growing her hair long. First it was shaggy and then the ends bent out like a Dutch girl's cap, and then she had a very stubby ponytail with bobby pins at the sides. No, she had not been *made* to grow her hair. It was an experiment she freely chose, and I should please not make it harder. I suspected her of hoping long hair could pick up spirit messages, but hell, maybe she just wanted to be a Real Woman.

The Gay Liberation Movement needed its history kept, so the photographer in me woke up and got busy. In the spirit of Mathew Brady, in black and white, I shot forlorn little bands picketing St. Patrick's Cathedral, or chaining themselves to the mayor's gate, or being leaned on by police horses, or being pushed into paddy wagons. Also a hundred plain brave faces that had stopped pretending. Also sweet love shining bright. Gentle mouths. Bright eyes. Light along a cheek.

I meant to turn Vera's room back into a darkroom and make archival prints, but Beck came to live with me. There were disadvantages. She took that room, and she slowed me down on Bar-None. "Lives with her daughter" doesn't sound much more inviting than "lives with her ex-lover," but I didn't care. I wanted Beck with me.

We had a pretty good life, though not upwardly mobile. Beck signed up with a temporary agency and went wherever it sent her. She demonstrated hair dryers and vegetable peelers and needle threaders. In plaid kilt and tam, she posed as a Scottish sex symbol — feeling, she said, more like the Salvation Army — and passed out handbills urging passersby to be Scot-like thrifty at a new bank. She did some typing for a poet who liked strikeovers because he wanted his letters to look human instead of mechanical. He was putting together a reading tour. "Professor Dull Dull, Dull College, Dullsville, Dull State, Dear Professor Dull." She cooked for a low-budget film crew out on location and fetched wigs and theatrical blood. Evenings, Beck played her guitar and sang her little folk repertoire — "Shorty George," "East Virginia," "O Lula!" "The Frozen Logger," "A Maid Again I Ne'er Will Be" — and wrote letters to Kurt.

And I worked on Bar-None. It was hard. I'm always amused by straight women who think they have only to decide to have a little lesbian fling and hundreds of eager dykes will present themselves. I may, and one middle-aged administrative assistant may ask you to dance, if you're beautiful. The rest of them would like to know you a little better.

I took Ap-Fu women home sometimes, and had long talks and short goodnight kisses. It was a lot like taking Ardith home, except that sometimes one would stay. I never could lure anyone into staying, but if I touched her hair and she leaned her head against my hand, I knew she had decided in advance to stay. Decided earlier in the day.

She would be someone determined to participate in the Sexual Revolution and break out of her old too-serious nest-building ways, never dating, never playing, waiting and waiting for Ms. Right. She would be someone working on Bar-None.

Some gay people posed as respectable to get into the governor's office and then refused to leave until he promised to work for gay rights, a cold day in hell. They went to trial for trespass. Beck and I went down to Centre Street to demonstrate outside the courthouse. We marched in a not very big, not very frightening circle inside a pen made of gray police sawhorses. There were TV cameras. There were cops watching us, and people with Civil Liberties Union armbands watching the cops so they wouldn't smash our heads.

I considered myself a pretty good chanter, past all ladylike reserve, but Beck was of a different and higher order. She had screamed at the Pentagon Building, commanding it to heal itself. She had screamed at the harsh Chicago cops even as they arrested her. This little gay protest could have seemed beneath her, a waste of her skills, but she was never a snob. She pitched her voice high and let loose. The idea, she said, was to sound like a banshee, and I think maybe she came close. She was much smiled upon. No one had seen anyone like her before. Naturally she lost her voice. She said protesting didn't count otherwise.

An old lady asked a cop what was going on. "Who are these *people?*" she asked, and on being told we were homosexuals said, "This should not be permitted."

"They got a right, ma'am," he said. "They got a right."

Beck was impressed. "He's a decent person. I can't believe it," she whispered in her lost voice. "The cops in Chicago really are pigs."

The old lady, much distressed, said, "But can't you see they're all paid agents of Russia and China?"

"They got a right," he said, and she wrote down his badge number.

Across Brooklyn Bridge came *another* march, much bigger than ours and dressed as for church—suits and dresses, hats. Those marchers were singing "The Son of God Goes Forth to War" with crazy eyes. I remembered Jesus whipping the money-changers. I remembered the Spanish Inquisition. Had these sincere zealots heard the Voice of God telling them to clean up Sodom and Gomorrah?

"Walt Whitman!" I yelled. "Gertrude Stein! Help us!"

And that Christian horde went right past us, up Lafayette Street and away. They hardly looked at us.

It's all in who you know.

I watched the news scared that night. We wanted coverage, of course, so other gay people would start telling themselves, "I should be there," and next time we wouldn't be so sparse and pitiful. On the other hand, I wanted to keep my job. Millicent was very intolerant of anything that called dubious attention to our office. The unwritten code was, do it and shut up. I was not on the six o'clock news. At eleven I went to the bathroom, and when I came back Beck whispered, "Guess who was on TV."

But nobody told Millicent and she didn't believe

in owning a TV set, so I got through one more time. You screw your courage up to come out and you're not out after all. You have to do it again and again.

Beck flew back to Kurt because it was his birthday.

Charles brought Laurel back from California in his car. I took a vacation day. He silently carried her backpack upstairs and left. They looked wonderfully sick of each other. Laurel was, in fact, sick, with urinary frequency, and went to the bathroom without saying hello.

I gave her uva ursi tea and lots of water. "You know what causes frequency, don't you? Fucking," I said, unjustly; I'd had it myself a while before, which is why I had some uva ursi on hand.

She lay on the couch getting well, talking. Charles, she said, had stayed with her and Miles a long time, too long, until Miles asked him to leave. Charles was a fairly good lover, she said — in the morning, before a day in the car together made them hate each other.

I still wanted the uncensored contents of her head, and I knew I had to listen to this distasteful stuff in order to get the rest.

Laurel said, "Once at a gas station he pounded on the restroom door to make me hurry. I didn't speak to him all day. This country is so beautiful, even with Charles."

Now we're getting there, I thought.

She said, "I've flown across it so many times

without seeing it, except once the sky was clear all the way and I saw the plains become foothills and then mountains. It was so orderly. Everything fit together. The Black Hills are really black. But a car's the right way to see everything. I thought about the Indians the whole way. Do you know what's scary? They have a dance that's going to make all the white people fall into a hole in the earth. Of course that's only fair, but on the other hand, I'm white."

I said, "It sounds like a white plot. 'Now don't you fuss and don't you raise hell, you just go out in the desert and dance in a circle and pretty soon Whitey will disappear down a hole.' "

She said, "I thought about the pioneers, too. All those bones they left. It was so sad. The deserts are so wide. The mountains are so steep, and the pioneers had no superhighway. Nevada was endless. No place to pee. Not even a bush. And then right at the edge of Nevada was a beautiful casino made of oak and stained glass, and a *very* beautiful restroom. What did the pioneers do? They were babies and menstruating women and pregnant women and there wasn't any casino for them. I put a quarter in the slot machine to say thanks. Then we looked off to the east and there were the Bonneville Flats, this immense flat plain of salt, and I thought of all the little white-topped wagons coming across."

I said, "They were too soon. They should have waited for the railroad. They knew it would come. The land was no good to them without it. But they wanted to be first and get the best."

She said, "There was room for everybody. It's still mostly empty. They had this fantasy of Sea-to-

Shining-Sea. They did all that to the Indians for a fantasy, when there was room for everybody. I'm glad I'm home."

I didn't want to mention right then that we shouldn't have taken Manhattan, either, though we did put it to good use as a refuge for the people the rest of the country didn't want.

She said, "I want to get all the homosexual shit out this time."

But not with me, I knew. It was all right. She loved me, there was no reason to doubt. But she didn't desire me in any way. My heart ached a little, but I had no sexual feeling for her either, or even any need to kiss her.

I said, "There are a lot of women at Ap-Fu who will be glad to hear that. And of course there's Beck."

"Charles and I quarreled over Beck for hundreds of miles. He wants her too."

"Charles can keep his filthy mitts off Beck!" I yelled.

Laurel laughed and fell asleep. I looked at her a long time, thinking, "Has any other watchman stiller stayed to the smiting of this gong?" not right then feeling the gong very much. My main desire was to hold Laurel against my bare skin and make her well, and that's not the kind of desire that drives you crazy, at least not right away.

That evening some of us Ap-Fu women went uptown to a lecture by a couple of shrinks who claimed to be curing lesbians. The shrinks believed oppressing lesbians was correct because it motivated us to struggle harder to be straight. They called lesbians vampires and cannibals, for making the usual mistakes everybody makes. Lesbians alone in all the world were supposed to be too sane and healthy for that. They said we preyed on young women and spoiled their chances for a good life. They were perfectly serious in their nonsense. They didn't know how likely a young woman was to be sent home in a cab if she seemed a little nervous. We told the shrinks, "In five years, the women you have cured will come to Ap-Fu — but by then they'll have kids."

I hurried home, afraid Laurel would be gone. She was still there, still resting on the couch but already much better, with her beauty back, Charles evaporated.

She said, "I'd like to stay with you a couple of months, if that's okay."

"Of course it's okay," I said.

"I was shy about asking," she said.

"I was shy about inviting you, but I trusted you to know you're welcome."

"I have more confidence in you than anybody else," she said.

I had no confidence in her, but felt willing to be exploited if she wanted to. I even showed her where the money was hidden, saying, "I can't bear to think of you going around New York with nothing in your pocket but a subway token."

"I have two subway tokens and forty dollars and I'll get a job," Laurel said. "Someone who likes my build will say I have a nice telephone voice and hire me."

When I got home from work next day, Laurel was

cooking. I sat in the kitchen doorway enjoying the sight of her. She said she wanted to do grocery shopping, cooking, and dishwashing as her share.

"That's too much," I said. "What would you get in return?"

"I want to pay a third of the rent, too," she said.

I said, "That's not fair. You won't have a room of your own or a private place to see your friends."

Then Jeff came. Jeff the handsome Columbia student. We ate Laurel's good supper — eggs in cheese sauce — and then I went to Ap-Fu. It was very important to me to have things to do.

I took a handsome woman named Doris home with me, so I didn't care that we met handsome Dennis on the stairs.

I wonder if Doris made Laurel jealous. It didn't occur to me at the time. At the time I was mystified. Why was kind and lovely Laurel talking like this, as though to drive me nuts?

About sex with Charles, in the most dismaying detail, preferred positions, depth of penetration, Oneida-type experiments.

I said, "You're not a virgin anymore. Virgins choose."

"My body chose Charles," Laurel said. "When he touched me, I knew my body was going to choose him."

I said, "What bullshit! Women used to claim great love and now they claim great lust. When they're thirty-three they finally tell the truth — 'I was lonely and I wanted people to like me' — but when you're twenty-three you still talk bullshit."

"Charles is jealous of you, too," Laurel said.

I said, "I can't think why."

She also, out of nowhere, talked about the hypermammary administrative assistant. "She was too old. Her skin wasn't nice. Dennis and I are going to Nova Scotia tomorrow. For three weeks. Why do people always hurt each other?"

"There's always somebody waiting to feel hurt no matter what we do. Hurt by how we wear our hair. Hurt because we don't do our wash on Monday. Whatever. If they can't stand the heat they should get out of the kitchen," I said, wondering if I would be able to get out of the kitchen since clearly I could not stand the heat, and when I stood quite a lot of heat the king commanded that the kitchen be heated seven times hotter.

Laurel politely left me alone with Doris.

I said, "How would you like to sleep in the same bed with Laurel and keep your hands off her?"

Doris said, "I would strive to make her see it was not in her interest for me to keep my hands off her."

"I don't know how," I said.

"Not your hands. Mine. Shouldn't be off her," Doris said.

She gave me a full warm kiss but did not want to stay. She left and Laurel came back to the couch.

Did Laurel want me to command her not to go to Nova Scotia? Did she want not just to depress me and drive me away but to enrage me? Force me to make wild noises about Charles and sexual experiments?

Those would come later, when she found my fight point. Now she was only at my flight point.

I asked my faithful Chinese companion, the oracle book I Ching, what to do. "Be dependable," it said. "Be virtuous. Teach." I had to laugh.

I said, "It's all too deep for me, too much for me, too mysterious for me. I don't know anything."

I went to bed. Laurel stayed on the couch, not far away, though Beck's room and bed were available.

"Why is Charles jealous of me?" I asked.

"Oh — " Laurel said.

I waited a long time for the answer but there was just that oh.

I said, "I have loved you pretty good, for me," and shut my bedroom door.

The night chilled down. I hoped the cold might drive Laurel to my bed, but then my conscience smote me and I put a blanket over her.

CHAPTER FIVE: THEN

Along came Peg, an ardent and gentle lover. She was a writer of soft-porn novels, all heterosexual. "Because," she said, "porn has to be dirty — and nothing lesbians do is dirty." Peg knew nothing about heterosexuality, having been a steadfast butch from earliest childhood. "I was really surprised to grow up to love women," she said. "I never liked girls. If you threw a ball at a girl, she'd cry or something."

Peg's publisher wanted kinky. "More kinky, more kinky," he told her, sternly, as though correcting a moral failure. He gave her lump payments, no royalties. If she wrote fast enough she could make $2,000 a year. On that and odd jobs she lived in one room, share the bath, no phone, in a slum in outer Queens not handy to the subway, and ate a lot of pasta. She was nice and plump.

She was low on kinky ideas and scared. Would she have to write a real book someday and not make any money at all?

She made my toilet tank stop running just by tightening something. She brought glass and replaced a cracked windowpane. I considered her homeless. I asked her to move in.

"Are we moving too fast?" she asked.

"Yes," I said.

But I really liked Peg, and I was in a hurry. Laurel would be coming back from Nova Scotia. I was afraid to be without distraction. Peg moved in.

It was so great to have plenty of sex, nothing rationed or careful, everything abundant — though maybe a little ritualized.

She had heard of sexual problems and wondered what they might be. We had some, naturally.

She'd had dozens of lovers and expected me to defer to her expertise. I would not.

I wanted the light on. She wanted it off.

She wanted simultaneous orgasms. I wanted to take turns and watch. She didn't feel beautiful enough to be watched.

She accused me of holding back, and of course I did; if I let her know I liked something she would stop it at once and move on to cunnilingus. Holding back was the only way I could hang on to the simple good stuff, hugs and kisses.

She thought cunnilingus was the absolute living

crazy-making end, the beyond-which-nothing. I thought it was a little ho-hum, and besides it kept us from looking into each other's eyes. How could I know she loved me if I couldn't see her eyes?

I thought hand-fucking was a sad imitation of the hets and wanted none of it. Peg said nonsense, it's not an imitation of anything, it's a really thrilling original act of its own. The cervix likes it, the clit likes it, there's a place behind the pubic bones that likes it. "Do you really not like it?" she asked.

"Give me a minute. Yes, I like it," I said.

It's not so bad to have sexual problems if there's plenty of time and energy and privacy to work on them, but Beck flew back. Peg and I had to stay in the bedroom with our sexual problems and work on them there. No more naked breakfasts, no more panda cries, but good old Peg claimed not to mind. "I always wanted a family," she said.

We were a nice family, the working poor. Beck turned out to have a dirty mind so she was able to help Peg with her work by doing kinky-thought brainstorms.

"How about this? — a guy goes to a potency clinic. How about this? — a guy's on a bus at night and hears all this slurping and it's wall-to-wall blow jobs. How about this?" and Peg would cry, *"Yes!"* and start bashing away at her typewriter and have ten pages by bedtime.

I could never handle porn myself. It stayed in my mind and degraded my love life. But Peg was a pro, like a gynecologist. That stuff didn't turn her on. Maybe some of her detachment came through and that was what upset her publisher.

Laurel came back from Nova Scotia. She fit right

in. She even helped Peg with some kinky thoughts. She put money into the kitty without being asked and kept the kitchen clean. Of course the rest of us cleaned it sometimes, too. As women, we understood how fast you can become a burned-out case in a kitchen.

Peg liked Laurel without being excessive. Beck seemed not to fall in love with Laurel, and when I asked why she told me, "I wouldn't know how to touch such a woman." Maybe that was what held Peg back, too. Laurel couldn't get simple and shabby enough to stop being one of the world's great beauties. I wondered how *I'd* managed to touch her. It felt so good to be past all my old-foolism, solid with Peg, calm, comfortable, simply fond of Laurel, with no further illusions about bridging Generation Gap.

Fall came on, cold nights and warm clothes. One night Beck and Laurel came in late, fresh and cold and beautiful, leaned over our bed, offered icy cheeks to kiss, and ran away laughing.

Peg said, "You really had quite a thing going, didn't you?"

"It was all in my head," I said. "Mainly, I hated being divided from Laurel, and now I'm not."

"Wow! Did you need me!"

"She just likes to flirt. Don't hold it against her. They'll be lovers in a few days."

I loved seeing Beck get along with a sister. She resented her actual blood-born sisters and longed to be an only child. I mean, as a little girl she did. *Fred's* only child, to be exact. I had one-two-three-four little Daddy Freaks in a row — such a surprise to me, a Mama-Freak who until then thought Freud was crazy. When Fred remarried, his new wife got the mother resentment, and I became a mere person, no longer archetypal and gigantic. I had to rise or fall on my own merits.

So Beck was my friend, and Laurel was the sister Beck could cheerfully share with and help and laugh with and tear around town with, and I was sort of their mama, a little bit.

One morning very early, Peg came back from the bathroom all hushed and glowy, saying, "There's something you've got to see."

Never a willing riser, I grumbled, "What?"

"You'll see. Come on."

I stumbled after her making my morning groans, muttering, "This better be good." She led me to Beck's open door, and stepped back with a little bow and a hand-sweep of presentation.

There they were, Beck and Laurel naked in each other's arms and legs, asleep with their faces tilted up, heroic and noble and serene and angelic and eternal and goddess-like, their glossy red and glossy dark hair mixed together on the flowered pillow, a flowered sheet around their hips, so beautiful, so beautiful.

I suppose if the Virgin Mary had manifested, I would have done the same thing—I ran for the camera. The film was slow so the shutter was slow and loud. It woke them up but they didn't care.

"I left the door open so you'd do that," Beck said.

"We'll leave now and shut it," I said.

They hadn't come out when I went to work. Peg, writing at home, saw nothing of them. She phoned me mid-afternoon to say, "They're still in there. I think they're stuck together." Even though I had forbidden her to call me at work, she knew I'd like to hear that.

And, yes, I liked it, and wondered why. There were so many reasons not to. Your child should not be sexual, not where you can see her anyway. Certainly she should not be sexual with someone you've had a tender two hours with and are just barely escaping crying about. I remembered jealousy, that horrible pain and disease. Where was it? I didn't want it, but where was it? Why was I not feeling an appropriate emotion? Had my gray plastic grown back? No, my heart felt very warm and alive, overflowing. Was I crazy? Hold that thought.

Laurel decided to stop being a dabbler — a little art, a little music, a little history, a little literature — and prepare to support herself. Which of her minor gifts should she bring to majority? She and Beck discussed it tirelessly and ended up with psychology. Laurel should become a shrink, a wounded healer. It really was a good idea. We drank to it.

They were lovely together, gentle and quiet with heightened pink faces, drawing each other, cutting each other's hair and huffing the snippets away. Leaning together at the table, they went through Beck's childhood drawings and paintings, the whole brown accordion file of them, slowly. It took them a week, because Laurel really looked, really felt Beck's tiny confident paw being bold with line and splash. Laurel still cooked, but now it was with Beck against her, kissing the little nick the paring knife made, following her from stove to refrigerator to counter. They learned the names of each other's relatives. They sang, even though Laurel said oh no she couldn't. Beck insisted. And Laurel was right — she couldn't sing, but the soft flat bleat she produced made Beck's face melt.

Those were the good parts. The bad part was the phone. Charles forgot the tedium of his cross-country drive and began again to hanker. Beck tried to be modern and ungrasping. "I don't *want* to cling," she said. "I don't *want* to bitch and complain. I want to open my hand and let her fly away without a single feather even *bent.* But Charles is a *vampire.* He *drains* her. Why does she let him? Can't she see?"

I was pleased, because until then Beck bawled me out for saying stuff like that. In me it was old-timey shit.

Laurel would come back from talking with Charles so diminished, so tired. I suspected her of feeling guilty — as though she owed that creep something. Once again he mewled and puked at her until she said yes, he could come down for a little while.

"That bloodsucker! That ghoul!" Beck whispered to Peg and me. To Laurel she turned an untroubled face, modern, unpossessive.

Peg and I went out for the evening. When we came back, Laurel and Charles were sitting on the stairs outside our door. We went inside. Beck's door was closed.

I began to be afraid Laurel was going to play Beck as she had played me. I began to be angry at Laurel.

In a little while she came in. Beck's door stayed shut. Laurel and Peg and I talked softly in the kitchen.

Laurel said, "I'm so confused."

"Go with your real wish," I said. "Follow your crotch."

"My crotch is conditioned to be straight."

"Be straight, then."

"It's so beautiful with Beck. I even do things. And I don't wash my hands all day. But I may not have the guts to choose what I really want."

"What do you really want?" Peg asked.

"Beck. I want Beck," Laurel said, unfirmly.

I said, "But Beck's going to hug orphans, and Charles is going to make a lot of money in the big hairy man's real world."

"Please don't be angry. Don't be sarcastic. I really am confused, and I really can't help it."

The next day, a Sunday, Beck went out — a game that two could play at. Laurel spent the day making a sun top for her out of a piece of tan and gold cloth. "I have to see this next to Beck's hair," she said. Whenever Peg and I got up and stumbled to the bathroom or the refrigerator, we found Laurel still poking awkwardly away, refusing a thimble, getting her fingers bloody. It hurt to see her.

And then Beck was home again and Laurel was holding the strange little garment against Beck's shirt with tender critical concentration, like a master seamstress capable of any desired amendment. The fit was zero, but the color did look good with Beck's red hair.

In the night, Beck left Laurel sleeping and came to the living room. Peg and I were bobsledded on the couch watching television, but we turned it off and listened to Beck.

She said, "I've never felt anything like this before. I have no vocabulary for it."

Peg said, "That's because there is no such vocabulary."

Beck said, "How could going to bed change everything? She was my dear friend, and now she's something I don't have a word for. I'm not exactly lustful. I don't know what to call it. And I feel possessiveness coming on, but is it really, or is it just that I don't want that slimy Charles near her? I didn't mind about Dennis. Did I? I don't *think* I did. And I don't like living so close with her here. It's like she's cornered into bed with me. I've faked so much in my life. I know what faking feels like. I can't stand to think of Laurel faking with me, or doing anything she doesn't really want to. And how do I know it's me she loves instead of you? The you that's in me? The part of me that's you?"

In fact, I had been very much liking the idea that Laurel was loving me in Beck. Beck an unblemished me of the right age. Luckily I hadn't said so.

"I think Laurel can tell us apart," I said. "You should have seen Laurel's face while she worked on that weird little garment for you. It said she's sorry she went out with Charles. She's sorry she kept you waiting."

"It did?" Beck said. "I thought it said, 'You look great in tan and gold.' "

"That too," I said.

CHAPTER SIX: THEN

Laurel came back from the phone looking rosy and pleased. Flattered. "Miles wants me to come home," she said.

I said, "Will you?"

"Not right away," she said.

Beck said nothing.

I was so angry. How could Laurel even consider going back to Miles, leaving Beck? Laurel came into and out of our life according to how angry she was at Miles. Beck and I were incidents in her lovers' quarrel with him. But I didn't say that.

I was angry because Laurel didn't go to bed when Beck did, and I didn't say that either.

"What about studying psychology?" I asked.

"Oh, I can do that out there, if I decide to."

"I thought you had decided to."

"Nothing with me is ever definite," she said.

Peg and I went to a lesbian bar, dancing and drinking to enrich the Mafia. We spent too much, and resolved never to do that again. I bought a jug of cheap wine on the way home. We sat and talked with Laurel and Beck and drank it in what I hoped were sips.

But I woke up with the fear so familiar to drunks, that I had done something awful and forgotten it.

I was lying face-down on the bed. I had a terrible headache. Peg came in.

"Has she gone?" I asked.

"Yes."

"Fuck her! Fuck her! Fuck her!" I sobbed, over and over.

Beck came in. I braced myself for reproach, but she was gentle, loving, and serene.

I said, "I'm sorry I messed it up for you."

"You didn't," Beck said.

"I'm sorry I drove her away."

"She'll be back," Beck said.

I stayed home from work, sick. Beck told me what happened the night before.

"You told her she exploits people," Beck said.

"Oh, God," I said.

"She said she only exploits people who go limp and say, 'Exploit me! Exploit me!' and you blushed like a beet. Did you say that to her?"

"It amounted to that," I said.

Beck said, "You said it didn't matter what she did to *you,* but by God don't play with *me.* You said you knew she didn't care for you or what you thought, and that made her run to the phone and call Charles. You went to bed, very slow and stately and drunk. Sailed. Very angry. You thought she had rejected my love. But I'm not in love with her."

"You're not? You sure had me fooled."

"I told you. I don't know the words. You should listen. I do know the words 'in love.' It's something else. I'm just as confused and doubtful as Laurel. You don't know how hard it is to give up the protection and prestige and money and power of men, especially when maybe you don't have to. Maybe you're straight, or near enough."

"I do know. I didn't do it myself until I knew I'd die if I didn't. And who knows, maybe you won't die," I said. "But, the fact is, men can't protect us. We are all, men and women together, protected by an orderly society. And hardly any of them have any money, either. Almost all women have to work. Both of your grandmothers supported their families. You could find giving men up ain't so tough. When it comes time to give them up or die."

Beck said, "Do you want philosophy or do you want to hear about Laurel?"

"Laurel," I said, though philosophy was impersonal and Laurel was about me being a drunk with amnesia, a thorough embarrassment.

Beck said, "She cried and cried while she waited

for Charles to come get her. She didn't see why you were afraid she might hurt me, but not afraid I might hurt her. Why weren't you worried about her too? I tried to explain that you couldn't possibly love her as much as me, because I'm your own. Your own self."

"Right," I said. Was seeing how much I cared for her what kept Beck so calm? The weird wild dyke ma had maternal instincts after all. How about that?

"Bone of your bone," Beck said. "She feels pressured to be a lesbian. It hurts her that you can't love her if she isn't. But you can love me if I'm not. I told her it's because I'm bone of your bone."

Peg came home paint-spattered from an odd job. She said, "I was really upset. I had no idea you loved that kid that much. I mean, still love her. This minute. But I thought about it all day and I came to terms. You have to realize that under all her experience, Laurel is a scared little kid who needs you. You have to realize how, and how much, Laurel loves you and let that be enough. You have to do some inner growing and love her just as she is."

"Yes, ma'am," I said, pretty sure I couldn't. I had made such mighty efforts to love Laurel as she was, and she had made mighty efforts to make it harder and harder for me to do that.

Peg said, "And I have to realize how you love me."

"How?"

"Like bread and salt and water and air. Not magic. Not like an angel lit on your lip."

"Did I say that last night?"

"You did."

"Oh, God."

"And I have to realize how I love you."

"How do you love me?"

"Like glimpses into other people's houses, and bread and salt and water and air."

Laurel and Charles came by for her stuff. I fled to my room when I heard her key in the door but took myself in hand and went back and said, sturdily-kindly, "Hello, Laurel. Hello, Charles." She had her back to me, barely answered, maybe didn't.

Beck was laughing, happy, helping gather things. She took Laurel's fifty-dollar bill out of the hiding place and tried to give it to Laurel, but she wouldn't take it.

I went back to my room. Laurel came to use the phone. I should have given her some privacy, but I didn't want to be near Charles. She called Miles and spoke very softly.

I heard almost nothing. It was almost privacy, except that I did hear her say she had to get out of New York because she'd had something sexual with everybody but Seth and it was just too complicated.

In a little while I heard the front door close. I went out. Beck was arranging three red dahlias in a water glass, saying, "Laurel brought these. She said, 'These are for you,' but I didn't know if that was singular or plural. I guess it was plural, since there are three of us. She still doesn't see why you're not afraid I'll hurt her."

"How could you hurt her?" I said. "You love her."

"How could she hurt me? She loves me."

"But she's going back to Miles. She's clobbering you."

"That doesn't clobber me. After all, I love Kurt."

I said, "I was afraid she had split you open in the

peculiar way a woman can split you open, and left you to put yourself back together as best you can."

"No," Beck said. "That didn't happen."

I said, "Well, if that particular nerve wasn't touched in you, then there's no problem."

"That's what I've been telling you. There's no problem."

I wrote Laurel a note, saying I was sorry I hurt her. I said I didn't know how to love but I had loved her as well as I was able. I said I hoped she would stay with us again and that we could talk again. I had to mail the note to her in care of Charles.

Beck and Laurel talked on the phone. Beck told me some of what they said.

"I asked her if she'd believe you love her if you told her so, and she said no, she'd think it was just sex. Anyway she cares nothing for love. What she wants from you is liking and understanding."

I felt that Laurel was rejecting the only thing I was good at and asking for a tip-toe stretch. She was like my mother-in-law who liked me best when I sang soprano and wrecked my throat.

Laurel came to dinner, pale and convalescent. She'd been sick for several days. Had she caught Charles' disease?

She was sick but not closed or silent. We pleasantly ate Beck's good dinner. Laurel got hiccups and Beck held her astride and rubbed her back and healed them. All so sweet.

Then the doorbell rang. "Fuck fucking Charles!" I said. When he came in I said, "Hello, Charles."

"Oh, what a hypocrite!" Laurel said. "A second ago you were saying, 'Fucking Charles!'"

Charles was unmoved. What did he care as long as she spent the night in his bed?

Peg slipped the fifty into Laurel's coat pocket and Laurel left with it unawares.

In a little while she phoned. "You bitch," she said. "You put the money in my pocket."

"Yes," I said. "Can we talk about our other differences?"

"We can try," Laurel said.

"I was mistaken and I'm sorry," I said. "I can't help interfering when I feel Beck is being ill-used. I attributed emotions to Beck that she won't know about for fifteen years. The only way you can be in relationship is to get away from me and my excessive joy and pain at what I imagine are your joys and pains. You two understand each other perfectly."

"Yes, we do," Laurel said.

I said, "The problem is in my projections. On top of not wanting Beck to be rejected, I identified with her. I felt you were sort of accepting me when you accepted Beck. So I took it sort of personally when you seemed to reject Beck too."

Laurel said, "You didn't need to be accepted vicariously. I had already accepted you, yourself, directly."

I said, "You went to some pains to tell me you did not accept me."

"When? How?" Laurel cried. "Haven't I been careful never to hurt you?"

"Oh!" I grunted, as though hit. "The question rouses in me a ball made of shit and snakes and bits of string and hair and I don't know where to take hold of it."

"Try," Laurel said.

"You rubbed my nose in Charles," I said. "You couldn't stop giving me excessive distasteful erotic detail. I disliked it so much. You must have meant me to dislike it. There was no way I wouldn't hate it. There was no way you wouldn't know I hated it."

"I thought it was interesting, and I always told you everything. Why should I stop? I knew you didn't like it, but it didn't mean I rejected you. I didn't like it either, but it was part of my life."

"I can't stand having you with Charles," I said. "He makes you sick. You're sick now."

"Maybe your attitude is what makes me sick. Maybe you make me sick."

"You know perfectly well I don't make you sick. I make you well. But okay. Next point. You said the administrative assistant was too old and her skin wasn't nice. I assumed you were telling me you don't like old ladies whose skin isn't nice."

"You're crazy! Lucille, you're so crazy! I never knew you were such a crazy lady! In the first place, your skin is nice."

I laughed.

"Okay, next point," I said. "I thought you weren't serious about me because I was wrong for you, and I knew I was wrong for you and it was okay. But then you weren't serious about Beck, even though she was right for you, and I knew it was because she's a woman. And that makes the problem political instead of personal, just as the radicals keep trying to make me see."

"But, Lucille, I wasn't serious about Charles or Dennis or any man either. Except Miles, a little."

"Of course! Of course!" I said, relieved. "I guess it's yourself you're not serious about. You could try valuing yourself as much as dogs value themselves. They'll go for miles, sniffing and agonizing, looking for the perfect shrine worthy of their sacred urine."

"I've noticed that about them," Laurel said. "I always thought they were rather foolish. I always thought it was rather superior of me not to fall into that. Oh, Lucille, we could have been having this conversation all along."

"You went to Nova Scotia."

"When I got back."

"I was with Peg then."

"Well," Laurel said, "I always loved you and told you so and it's not my fault you're crazy."

Dear Laurel, she did draw the poison out of me. I wondered what she'd say if she knew I was also her grandfather and her shrink and her witch friend and an old man she didn't know singing on the subway, even though I was in no way Charles.

Beck and her movie company went out to Long Island, shooting and doing other things I didn't ask about. She had hardly gone when Laurel called me, at work. "I'm going back to California tomorrow," she said.

I was instantly angry. How could she leave while Beck was out of town? But all I said was, "Um."

Laurel said, "I want Beck to come live with Miles and me."

"I think she'll want to," I said, feeling a little better.

"Can I come cook for you tonight?" she asked.

"No. We're going to Ap-Fu."

"I've been wanting to go there. Take me along."

"Okay," I said, but I got sick on the subway and decided not to go to Ap-Fu. Laurel made me invalid food and stayed home with me. Peg went to Ap-Fu alone.

Laurel and I sat the room's width apart. I was determined not to be critical or bossy or curious, so I was left with not much to say.

But I could not help myself. Looking as dull, sick, and withdrawn as possible, I said, "I couldn't possibly have understood you. You asked too much of me."

"I thought you did understand me."

"No, understanding is saying 'Yeah, yeah, yeah, I've done that, I've been there.'"

"There are other kinds of understanding," she said.

" 'Ah, I see, you were traumatized in infancy.' "

"You needn't polarize so. There are still other kinds," Laurel said.

"Name off some," I said, withdrawn and languid.

"There's recognition. Recognizing that certain things are there. A certain integrity, no matter how it looks. You could know I don't exploit people. I have real relationships. You could know that because I have a real relationship with you. It might not always be what the person wants, but it's real."

I saw her sneaking looks at the clock and told her, "Run along."

She said, "I just need to be back by ten in case Beck calls. I'll let you know if she calls."

"You needn't, unless she wants money or something. I'll just crash into bed the moment you leave," I said, yawning and bleary and totally no-pressure. I was quite proud of myself. Not a word about leaving in Beck's absence.

And the reward was that Laurel called. She said, "Beck doesn't need anything. She's coming to California with me."

"Ah," I said, much comforted. She did care for Beck. I said, "I'm sorry I was so awkward tonight. When I try not to be bossy I'm just mute."

"You're not really bossy," Laurel said, with a nice little laugh. "Some people have very strong opinions, and it's hard for some people whose opinions aren't that strong. You're so sure you know what Beck and I should do."

"But you're not so sure?"

"No. Neither of us is sure."

I said, "Maybe I don't understand you but Beck does, and she's all that needs to."

"Yes, she does," Laurel said.

I was enjoying a rainy evening alone, peacefully mending clothes, peacefully crying, when Beck and Laurel called, happy, giggling. "We're at Seth's. We're seeing colors," Laurel said. "Can you see them?"

"No, I can't see colors," I said. "I'm the wrong generation."

"We're taking off tomorrow. I want you to know we're well."

"Good."

"And happy."

"Even better."

"We don't know what we're doing."

"You don't need to."

"We'll be getting Beck's stuff while you're at work, so I wanted to say good-bye tonight. So 'bye."

" 'Bye. Enjoy California."

But they didn't go to California. They took a little bus trip and stayed with Laurel's friends here and there. I hoped the trip was to get to know each other, but maybe it was just because Beck hadn't traveled enough and needed to go somewhere.

And one night when Peg and I got home from Ap-Fu, there was Beck asleep on the couch in all her clothes. She woke half up, enough to say, "Laurel wants to cook for us tomorrow."

She phoned Laurel at Seth's next day to ask what food to buy and Seth told her Laurel was gone.

"She flew back to California last night," he said.

CHAPTER SEVEN: THEN

Beck sat on her bed and crocheted and crocheted. Hats and vests and granny squares. I told her she was crocheting a new little Beck, but she said none was needed. The old was intact.

Laurel, she said, was too difficult. Laurel got all hyper, like an overactive child, and wanted constant attention. Beck did not have the energy for that.

I thought, well, at least it wasn't my constant attention Laurel minded.

Laurel had a mean streak, Beck said. In that

gentle sweet voice she could say the awfulest things. For instance, she told Charles, "I just don't *like* you."

In such a good cause, a mean streak was acceptable.

Laurel was through with Charles, Beck said, and she also wanted to sever herself from all the other messy people, all the messes she made. Laurel actually said "sever." On their trip, Beck said, every friend they stayed with was one of the messes and all bleedy and sad-eyed and choked-up and putting out phony cheer.

I knew I was one of the messes. Beck must have known it too. Did she feel protective toward me as I did toward her?

I felt dull toward Laurel, pain-free, free of tears. It really helped to see Beck wasn't hurt. In fact, maybe she had hurt Laurel a little. That thought gave me a certain calmness. I liked it.

Beck went to hear Kate Millett speak in praise of bisexuality. No one else had ever said a good word for it, so Beck was excited and pleased. She could be her mixed-up self, it was okay. She could love women without getting clobbered and without getting stuck in some little by-way of life, because she could get along with men too.

"Bisexuality is a copout," I said.

"You lesbians are so tough. Here I am stretching and stretching, trying to reach *up* to my bisexuality, and you're calling it a copout."

"Sorry," I said, not sorry right then, but sorry on second thought. I was sorry I had spoken movement boilerplate rhetoric when a sincere person was trying to tell me something.

Beck and Peg got along fine but found me stingy, rigid, and bossy. We pooled our money, so they felt they'd been fair, but when I paid the bills I had to use a little of what Vera left me. I wasn't good at arithmetic, but clearly the number of months I could do that was finite.

I got so scared about money that I quit drinking, or thought I did. My temper got bad. I became a machine for shouting, "Turn off the lights! Don't heat a whole kettleful of water for one cup of coffee! Eat it up! Wear it out! Mend it! Walk!"

I became, in short, She Who Must Be Disobeyed. Beck and Peg ganged up on me. "You're so tightass! You're so petty!" they yelled. The money Vera left was more than they'd ever seen. What was the problem?

I saw, yes, there was no problem. They would go away.

Beck wanted to become a midwife, as a way of doing something for women. She would go west to study for that.

Peg and I were getting ready to part. She had begun to grant or withhold caresses according to how I behaved in the rest of our life. She mistook sexual surrender for surrender. Sometimes she was too smart for her own good. She would leave soon. Good butches were always in demand and could set their own terms.

The money would last until I could be in charge of my life again. I could live on whatever I had, but I had to be in control of it, the only hand on the faucet.

I relaxed, bought beer, became mellow, sang with

Beck. Peg, who couldn't resist shirts, bought a shirt and went back to her therapy group. Beck took karate lessons. It was all right. The money would last.

Vera had a hysterectomy. I was her family in the waiting room, the one who was told there was no cancer, and then I was her first visitor. Her ears looked nice and pink.

I walked to the hospital and back every day and got very tired because I still had to do everything else I would have done. Visits to Vera did not benefit the family, so I couldn't use them to get out of family jobs like washing dishes and sweeping.

Peg was steadily mad at me for visiting Vera, who had given in to the temptation to squelch know-it-alls and squelched Peg despite my asking for mercy. Expert squelching was one of Vera's most valued skills, and now and then she couldn't resist it.

Peg was also mad at me for not wanting to make love anymore. She thought I stopped because I no longer needed her as a buffer against Laurel. No, I stopped the night I saw rage in Peg's face during an embrace. She was practically snarling.

I asked Peg to try not to be angry. Anger was spoiling the vibes in our home. She said she damn well could be angry. She considered her anger at me a great psychological achievement. It showed she was not some doormat puppy-dog wimp afraid to be angry when her cause was just. *She* wouldn't tiptoe around and bury differences just to keep the peace, like *some* people she knew. In fact, she said, she bragged about her anger to her therapy group. Sometimes shrinks give you a bum steer.

She felt quarreling was good. It cleared the air, it burned up the shit, it left her feeling expressed and purged and cheerful.

It left me hurt by all the unforgivable things she said, like "You're a sloppy drunk," and "You're the meanest son of a bitch I ever knew." Then, when I least could, she would want me to say everything was okay.

I said unforgivable things, too, like "I can't afford you," and "You talk too much." Her so-called writing had taught her to spread a little bit of material over a big space. "Guess what I saw today?" she liked to say, dramatically, and I liked to hide my eyes and gasp, crying, "No!" I'm afraid I called her writing so-called, too, but at least I didn't ask her to say everything was okay then.

Beck found Laurel's slippers under her bed. I bundled them up to mail and after much wavering back and forth added a note saying not to greet her might seem cold but I was embarrassed to be greeting her if I was one of the people from whom she wished to be severed.

She wrote right back. "Thank you for the note. Yes, no note would have been cold. I couldn't have borne no note."

She wrote that she loved me more than her own mother, and wanted to be loved more than Beck in return. So maybe being loved mattered to her after all? She wrote, "The only way I could stand your resentment was to pretend to be aloof, but I love you very much. You were right about Charles. Tell Beck I left without saying good-bye because I hated being weak around her. It is hard to forgive the ones who have seen us weak and coming apart, as you all have."

Peg read the letter. "Resisting lesbianism is making her sick," she said.

I said, "It may frighten you to hear just how megalomaniacal I am, but I feel that Laurel picked me out to be the one who can know and bear everything about her. She picked me out to be *God* — and kept testing me, so if I bore one hard thing the next would be harder."

"Nothing megalomaniacal about you can surprise me," Peg said. "But try 'mother' instead of 'god.' Miles is probably god. She wanted you to be the perfect mother who fills every need but needs nothing back."

I said, "Actually that's what I wanted, too. I was ashamed of myself for having needs when my ideal was to give and give. Why should I have such an ideal about her when I don't about anybody else?"

"You sure don't," Peg said, with an angry edge.

I didn't believe in altruism, mine or anybody's. That it even existed. But I felt bound to be altruistic toward Laurel.

Beck read Laurel's letter, quickly and aloofly, as though determined to be unmoved. She said, "It's falling apart. It's irrational. Nothing follows," and dropped it to the floor.

So despite her best efforts, Beck did have defenses. She knew how to blow a fuse instead of her whole power system.

Laurel was only, once again, flirting from the safety of three thousand miles, but would endure my living presence no better next time — if there was a next time. If she came again, she would run to Charles or someone again. She would never, I suspected, face the issues between us except from under somebody else's wing. And she would flirt with other people from under my wing and run to me when they made her mad.

Even so, I couldn't help responding to the love in her letter. And from a purely selfish point of view, wasn't it more wholesome and healthful, gentler on my gut, more in my own interest, to love her and feel tender toward her than not to?

I wrote her a note saying I was feeling very good toward her, glad I knew her, glad Beck knew her, sure of her love, sure of ours for her, but it was all sort of precarious and best not jiggled. So, I said, while it's at such a good place, let's leave it, and thanks for everything.

AFTERWORD: NOW

Laurel says she has a Master of Social Work degree and does psychotherapy. "It really is the solution to being loved without having to fuck," she says. "You were very smart. As a matter of fact, everything you told me was true."

In that case, I wish I could remember more of what I told her.

I say, "Let's see — I told you Charles was poison for you."

"Yes. I was pregnant when I left you and Beck so abruptly. He thought he could trap me with that, but

I had an abortion. It was all right. It wasn't horrible. He's rich now, he designs computers."

I say, "I was afraid the Baby Boomers would forget Western Civilization, but the little snots were only planning to replace it with something that would bewilder me. They would leave me a stranger in my own world. Every machine I own is obsolete. They even sent my record collection the way of the horse collar. Even 'Drums of Passion.' "

Laurel said, "We were such a big generation. There were so many of us. We knew we could really change things, and we did. I wish it had been for the better."

"I may not like everything now," I say, "but I wouldn't go back. You made a whole bunch of pains and indignities optional. White gloves and girdles and slips and high heels and narrow skirts you can't take an adult step in, and difficult foods designed to make you show you have no manners, and sexism and racism and girls forbidden to study woodworking and boys forbidden to study cooking, and pin curls, and lips and fingernails painted bloody. Lipstick all over your cup, all over your lover. Give me a minute and I'll think of some more. They're still around but now they're optional, so thank you. Never get so discouraged you forget your good deeds. And Charles would have made you rich now too. How do you feel about missing that?"

Laurel says, "For me to be rich would have been an accident. Not part of my natural life course. Marrying Charles was one mistake I managed not to make."

"Did you marry Miles?"

"Yes, briefly. And another one. A boy who had

never suffered. He was so sweet and babylike. Once-born. Everybody should know one of those, for a little while. Right now I'm single. And I have a burning question to ask you."

"Ask."

"I'm sorry to risk our delicate balance."

"It's okay," I say. "Everything is safely The Past. Behind the door. Over. At peace. Merely interesting."

"How did your second adolescence go?"

I say, *"That's* your burning question?"

"No, but it starts it."

"It was much like the first," I say. "But shorter."

"I'm as old now as you were then, and I'm thinking the same."

"You want a second adolescence? But your first was okay. You did all the rebel stuff. All the sexual stuff."

"Yes, but now I want an adolescence like yours."

"*Mine?* Mine was awful. Both of them were."

"Maybe they felt awful, but they were correct."

I say, "You want to be lonely and off-putting and rude and sullen and go for long solitary walks and talk to yourself and wish on the evening star?"

"Yes!"

"You want acne? You want to be constantly embarrassed and unsure? Afraid you stink? Afraid there's menstrual blood on your backside?"

Laurel says, "No, I want the good part. The good part is practicing your recorder all summer and crying at movies and memorizing poems and bringing such a big stack of books home from the library every week that your brother is ashamed to have you walk past his girlfriend's house with them."

"Did I tell you that?"

"No, I'm going by my brother. He would have been."

"Mine was," I say.

Laurel says, "And I'd rather not be the one who introduces promiscuity to my high school."

"I would have done that," I say. "I wasn't innerly virginal. But no one tempted me."

"Lately I've been doing only what tempts me, sexually," Laurel says.

I say, "I mean, what tempted me was not available. The second adolescence was an improvement in that respect, at least. Thanks to living in a hotbed of dykes. When I finally got the hang of it. And then, crash, I fell in love and wanted only one."

"Is that the one you're with now?"

"No, Eileen is two or three later. She was willing to take a chance on me. It helped that I had long since gone to Alcoholics Anonymous and sobered up. She never knew me as that particular idiot, so she could really love me. When I bought the first car that was my very own, I was following her home in it and I fell a little behind and when I came up over the top of a hill and saw her crooked tail lights again, and knew she was seeing me, I felt this rush of love up at me, this relief and joy coming back at me as definite as wind or heat, and I said, out loud, 'What a difference when somebody really cares!' And it's been like that for many years now. I've been mysteriously calm and serene. You must remember how easily I cried. But since Eileen, I couldn't squeak out a tear even when my dear brother died. He was dear even though he thought I should dance and play tennis instead of read. He deserved a tear."

"Yes," Laurel said. "The Greeks believed the dead need our tears."

"I know. I believe in tears. I would if I could."

Laurel says, "What about going to bed with friends? Affection taking its natural course?"

"We believe in that, but we don't do it. We don't believe in monogamy, or ask for it, but we practice it. I am quite mystified. Maybe it's because country lesbians tend to."

Laurel says, "I want a short adolescence, and then I want to grow up. I want to be plain and simple and love one dear beautiful generous *sane* woman."

I say, "I think we're getting to the burning question."

"Yes. Where's Beck?"

I write down Beck's address and hand it to Laurel. She puts it in her pocket without looking at it.

She says, "You're not going to think this is the only reason I wanted to see you?"

"No. I'm not as crazy as I used to be."

"Your friends knew where you went, but not where Beck went. When it came time for me to ask around."

"She doesn't even have the same name," I say. "You could never have found her. She left New York a little after you did. She was afraid to go lest I fall off the ladder scraping the ceiling and nobody would find me. Peg was gone by then. I said, 'If I fall, I'll lie there and get well or die. No big deal.' Beck waited as long as she could and then she left. She met a nice young man who loves plants and music and that's her name now. Her unborn children took one look at him and began to yell, 'Daddy! Daddy!' There was no resisting them. He's perfect for them. Less so for her. She's a midwife now. A little wider than when you knew her. She's evolving into Earth Mother. Very strong. She does herbs and healing things with her hands. She fixed my knee. She fixed my thumb. Her problem is impatience. Which doesn't do in a midwife, of course."

"Or an Earth Mother," Laurel says.

"Right. The impatience is new. It's since a woman broke her heart. She had to go live alone to cope with that. Where she could be silent. Because the more your family sees you're out of gas, the more they howl for gas. When you're the Mama. When you're the Daddy, they think, poor Daddy, trying to be Daddy and Mommy both, let's be extra quiet and helpful and good."

Laurel says, "So Beck's alone learning to be patient. How that moves me!"

I say, "She has a little old car I call her Mouse Mobile."

Laurel says, "It's Dream Ambulance!"

I say, "It's her little Manchurian horse."

"Do we get another chance, Lucille? If the gods send you the best too soon, before you know it's best, before everybody else has revealed his inner dustiness, can you go back, or do the gods say tough luck, you had your chance and you blew it?"

"We get lots of new chances. Otherwise we'd all be dead, and some of us aren't. Thus proving."

She says, "I have a letter I write to Beck every day in my head. It starts, 'I'll never forgive myself if I don't try one more time to see if there's anything left for us.' Then I embellish it a little. Small variations. 'I never found again your open spirit, your trustingness. How natural you find the experience of the divine, how easily you bear the loss of walls. How beautiful your clear bright nutmeg-colored eyes and their steady gaze. How peach-like your butt. How thrilling your voice saying my name. Your fingertips listen. Your touch heals.' I've speeded many a slow day with the writing of that letter."

"Do you want to call her and tell her?"

"Oh, I'd be shy, blurting it out with no preparation."

"Well, you could call her and say how are you and see how that goes and work up from there."

"I don't want to run up your phone bill."

"It's a local call."

"Really! She lives here! That's different, then."

"She's not exactly *living* here. She's camping here, in the state park, in a tent, for solitude. The phone's in a booth near by. She always answers in case it's her kids. Let me see if she's there and wants some company."

"If it doesn't seem like intruding," Laurel says.

I want to say Beck's been asking for news of you every month since you left. "What do you hear from Laurel?" she asks, offhand, like how's the weather? When her period reduces her strength, she can't help asking.

I want to say Beck is sitting there beside the phone booth in the piney woods waiting for your call.

I want to say she never had a companion as good as you or pleasure like she had with you. She never fell into anyone else's eyes and heard the humming of eternity. Yours was the only eyelid or fingernail except her children's while they nursed that Beck couldn't take her eyes from.

I want to say Beck will have to pay child support, so she'll be poor for a long time. And the kids will be around a lot, so there won't be as much privacy as you'd like. A beautiful girl and boy who have never been lied to or told they don't feel what they feel. You'll find them interesting, I want to say.

She's out all night a lot, I want to say, sitting beside women in labor, nothing induced, just the slow long process that only midwives will put up with now. The doctors schedule birth between nine and five, but Beck waits all night while the baby finds its own way out.

But I'm not as meddlesome as I used to be, and I will say none of this. It is Beck's to tell. Would I tell it and leave her with nothing to say, just silence and a look?

A few of the publications of

THE NAIAD PRESS, INC.

P.O. Box 10543 • Tallahassee, Florida 32302

Phone (904) 539-5965

Toll-Free Order Number: 1-800-533-1973

Mail orders welcome. Please include 15% postage. Write or call for our free catalog which also features an incredible selection of lesbian videos.

LAUREL by Isabel Miller. 128 pp. By the author of the beloved *Patience and Sarah.*	ISBN 1-56280-146-5	$10.95
LOVE OR MONEY by Jackie Calhoun. 240 pp. The romance of real life.	ISBN 1-56280-147-3	10.95
SMOKE AND MIRRORS by Pat Welch. 224 pp. 5th Helen Black Mystery.	ISBN 1-56280-143-0	10.95
DANCING IN THE DARK edited by Barbara Grier & Christine Cassidy. 272 pp. Erotic love stories by Naiad Press authors.	ISBN 1-56280-144-9	14.95
TIME AND TIME AGAIN by Catherine Ennis. 176 pp. Passionate love affair.	ISBN 1-56280-145-7	10.95
PAXTON COURT by Diane Salvatore. 256 pp. Erotic and wickedly funny contemporary tale about the business of learning to live together.	ISBN 1-56280-114-7	10.95
INNER CIRCLE by Claire McNab. 208 pp. 8th Carol Ashton Mystery.	ISBN 1-56280-135-X	10.95
LESBIAN SEX: AN ORAL HISTORY by Susan Johnson. 240 pp. Need we say more?	ISBN 1-56280-142-2	14.95
BABY, IT'S COLD by Jaye Maiman. 256 pp. 5th Robin Miller Mystery.	ISBN 1-56280-141-4	19.95
WILD THINGS by Karin Kallmaker. 240 pp. By the undisputed mistress of lesbian romance.	ISBN 1-56280-139-2	10.95
THE GIRL NEXT DOOR by Mindy Kaplan. 208 pp. Just what you'd expect.	ISBN 1-56280-140-6	10.95
NOW AND THEN by Penny Hayes. 240 pp. Romance on the westward journey.	ISBN 1-56280-121-X	10.95
HEART ON FIRE by Diana Simmonds. 176 pp. The romantic and erotic rival of *Curious Wine.*	ISBN 1-56280-152-X	10.95
DEATH AT LAVENDER BAY by Lauren Wright Douglas. 208 pp. 1st Allison O'Neil Mystery.	ISBN 1-56280-085-X	10.95

YES I SAID YES I WILL by Judith McDaniel. 272 pp. Hot romance by famous author. ISBN 1-56280-138-4 10.95

FORBIDDEN FIRES by Margaret C. Anderson. Edited by Mathilda Hills. 176 pp. Famous author's "unpublished" Lesbian romance. ISBN 1-56280-123-6 21.95

SIDE TRACKS by Teresa Stores. 160 pp. Gender-bending Lesbians on the road. ISBN 1-56280-122-8 10.95

HOODED MURDER by Annette Van Dyke. 176 pp. 1st Jessie Batelle Mystery. ISBN 1-56280-134-1 10.95

WILDWOOD FLOWERS by Julia Watts. 208 pp. Hilarious and heart-warming tale of true love. ISBN 1-56280-127-9 10.95

NEVER SAY NEVER by Linda Hill. 224 pp. Rule #1: Never get involved with . . . ISBN 1-56280-126-0 10.95

THE SEARCH by Melanie McAllester. 240 pp. Exciting top cop Tenny Mendoza case. ISBN 1-56280-150-3 10.95

THE WISH LIST by Saxon Bennett. 192 pp. Romance through the years. ISBN 1-56280-125-2 10.95

FIRST IMPRESSIONS by Kate Calloway. 208 pp. P.I. Cassidy James' first case. ISBN 1-56280-133-3 10.95

OUT OF THE NIGHT by Kris Bruyer. 192 pp. Spine-tingling thriller. ISBN 1-56280-120-1 10.95

NORTHERN BLUE by Tracey Richardson. 224 pp. Police recruits Miki & Miranda — passion in the line of fire. ISBN 1-56280-118-X 10.95

LOVE'S HARVEST by Peggy J. Herring. 176 pp. by the author of *Once More With Feeling.* ISBN 1-56280-117-1 10.95

THE COLOR OF WINTER by Lisa Shapiro. 208 pp. Romantic love beyond your wildest dreams. ISBN 1-56280-116-3 10.95

FAMILY SECRETS by Laura DeHart Young. 208 pp. Enthralling romance and suspense. ISBN 1-56280-119-8 10.95

INLAND PASSAGE by Jane Rule. 288 pp. Tales exploring conventional & unconventional relationships. ISBN 0-930044-56-8 10.95

DOUBLE BLUFF by Claire McNab. 208 pp. 7th Carol Ashton Mystery. ISBN 1-56280-096-5 10.95

BAR GIRLS by Lauran Hoffman. 176 pp. See the movie, read the book! ISBN 1-56280-115-5 10.95

These are just a few of the many Naiad Press titles — we are the oldest and largest lesbian/feminist publishing company in the world. We also offer an enormous selection of lesbian video products. Please request a complete catalog. We offer personal service; we encourage and welcome direct mail orders from individuals who have limited access to bookstores carrying our publications.